D0341535

Breathing Underwater

Breathing Underwater

LU VICKERS

Breathing Underwater is a work of fiction. The characters
and evens in the novel are the products of imagination, and
any resemblance to real-life persons, or to actual events, is
unintended.

Excerpts from *Breathing Underwater* appeared in different forms
in *Apalachee Review, The Gay Community News, Kalliope, Salon,
Women on Women 3,* Joan Nestle and Naomi Holoch, eds.
Plume/Penguin, eds. Naomi Holoch, and in *Every Woman I've
Ever Loved,* Catherine Reid and Holly Iglesias, eds. Cleis Press.

07   08   09   10   a   10   9   8   7   6   5   4   3   2   1

ISBN 1-55583-964-9
ISBN-13 978-1-55583-964-2

BOOK DESIGN BY VICTOR MINGOVITS

For Jennifer

1

What Mama wanted in life was to cruise around Florida like a Yankee tourist in a Cadillac convertible, Jimmy Dolan at the wheel. She wanted to wear dark sunglasses and drape a parrot-green scarf over her shoulders to set off her red hair. She wanted to wear a short linen sundress stamped all over with pink flamingos. She wanted Monkey Jungle and Cypress Gardens. Weeki Wachee and Silver Springs. She wanted to be Miss Florida, to smile and wave a dreamy hand from her throne on a float made entirely of pink and white carnations. But Sissy Gardner walked away with the Miss Chattahoochee title and along with it all of Mama's dreams.

I saw the crackled photograph of Mama and Jimmy Dolan bunched up next to each other in a shiny black Buick, Jimmy Dolan sitting in the driver's seat squinting up at the camera, his blond hair slicked back. You could see dark little furrows where he'd raked the comb through his hair. He slung his arm around Mama. She curved her body toward the camera like a spindly green plant seeking light. She was sixteen, already had the devil in her eyes. Who knows what went wrong.

Jimmy Dolan ended up marrying Sissy, becoming a

state senator, and buying a silver Cadillac. Mama ended up marrying Dwayne Edwards and having three children, one right after the other. Two girls who were nothing like the girls she had imagined, and in between them a squirrelly little boy she said looked like Clark Gable. She drove a dinged-up Fairlane that smoked like a mosquito truck, and she worked at the Florida State Mental Hospital just like her mother and father had, cleaned up after crazy people, scrubbed their floors, emptied their bedpans, undressed them, gave them baths, fed them, put them to bed, listened to them cry, made sure they didn't run away. She said there were two differences between taking care of us and them: (1) She got paid to take care of them; and (2) They were more interesting.

There was never any telling what she was going to do or say. One afternoon she got so mad at James and me for shooting caps in the house that she pinched her nose against the sulfur smell and ran out the door barefoot. She climbed up the stair-step branches of the Magnolia tree in our backyard and disappeared. At suppertime, Daddy made me stand in the grass beneath the tree with a plateful of Mama's favorite fried bream, like she was a cat or something. Her long, slender feet dangled beneath a cluster of waxy green leaves and saucer-sized white flowers. I held the plate high above my head. I watched her toes for a sign. She finally did come down.

By the time I turned eleven I could read her like a weather map, and with about as much luck as Frank Pepper, our local weatherman. Around 2:30 I'd start wondering what mood she was going to be in when she got home from work. If she came home smiling, we'd be able to keep watching TV. If she squinched her eyes and touched her fingers to her forehead, it meant she was going to lie down and not get up for a while, and we'd *damn well better be quiet.* If she squinched her eyes, touched her head *and* cussed at us, it was going to be a long afternoon. She might go off on one of her tirades about how sorry we were, screaming so loud the neighbors pulled back their curtains to look out their windows. Or she might just sulk and go to bed crying. You never really knew.

But one summer day, she surprised all of us—even herself, I think. Me and James and Maisey were lounging on the couch watching *Dark Shadows* when she busted through the door at 3:05, her teeth already clenched. "Goddammit, this house is a mess; y'all just sit on your asses all day and wait for me to come home and clean up, dontcha?" She bobbed her head at the room as if to say, "Just look at it."

James didn't even move his eyes. His left hand was shoved deep into a bag of barbequed corn chips, his lap sprinkled with a confetti of crumbs, his chin dusted orange. I glanced around—the house looked fine to me. The linoleum was swept, the dishes done. I'd even straightened the rooster and hen pictures Mama'd hung over the couch, the ones she made by gluing fifty million seeds together—sunflower seeds, lentils, mustard seeds—the ones the roaches were slowly eating. James had knocked the pictures crooked, slamming a basketball against the wall.

I wondered what mess she was seeing that I couldn't see. The dead black flies on the windowsill? The pile of magazines strewn across the kitchen table? Dust bunnies under the couch? Maisey glanced over at me and raised her pale brown eyebrows while Mama dug an orange bottle of pills out of her purse, then tossed the purse up on the kitchen counter. "If y'all were monkeys I might consider myself lucky," she said, opening the bottle and popping a pill in her mouth. "I

3

could open my own tourist attraction. But you aren't, and to top it off, you're more trouble."

It was us. We were the mess that needed cleaning up. She stomped into her bedroom, then stomped out five minutes later barefooted, dressed in shorts, her red hair pulled back like the beauty queen she'd never be. She picked up her purse. "Go get in the damn car," she said, her voice loaded, "and don't break the fishing poles when you slam the door." At the sound of metal in her voice, James dropped the bag of chips and we flew out the door, a flock of gun-shy crows.

Uptown, Washington Street was still backed up with three-o'clock traffic from the shift change at the hospital. Mama inched the car along, drumming her fingers on the steering wheel. A cloud of blue smoke rose in the air behind us. Innertube, a clownlike man with a rubbery face, walked past carrying a big black tractor inner tube over his shoulder and swinging a bicycle tire around his arm like a hula hoop. He headed down the street toward the Dime Store. I wanted a life like that. He might've been a mental patient, but he got to do whatever he wanted. No one could tell him what to do because he was crazy.

Mama drove us past the Chattaburger down to the Riverview to pick up bait. While she waited for Wilder Watson to shake crickets from a shit-splattered cardboard tube into our cricket cage, James dug bottles of NuGrape soda and Orange Crush out of ice in the big red Coke cooler by the screen door. Maisey and I leaned over a damp concrete vat swarming with silver minnows, a fine cool spray of water freckling our faces. When she went up to pay, Mama picked up a can full of wigglers just in case the fish weren't biting crickets.

The screen door flapped shut behind us, and we piled back into the car. Once we hit the road to the lake, Mama drove fast, like she was trying to escape something. Longleaf pines whipped past the windows, a smear of green. The bamboo fishing poles vibrated in the wind like insect antennae.

She uncoiled as soon as we got to Lake Seminole and she could look out the dirty windshield at all that water reflecting the blue light of the sky. Water kept Mama sane. And we knew it. Water, water, water, water, water. Any kind of water: bathwater, dishwater, lake water, rainwater, ditch water. She just seemed different when she was near water. Calmer.

Her eyes softened. Her face relaxed. Her voice lost that hard metal edge.

We spilled out of the car and I squatted on the mud damp ground to pick up a half-crumpled paper cup. Water oozed through the brown thatch of grass. It was a watershimmering day—even the air smelled green. The pale blue sky was streaked with cirrus clouds; light sparkled the lapping waves. Three children, four cane poles varnished to a liquid-brown shine, fishing string translucent as angel hair, gray metal hooks sharp as ice picks. A mother who needed water.

Clutching the cup, I ran to the other side of our little peninsula where fishermen docked their boats when they came in off the lake. Mama propped my pole up on the bank, holding hers and trying to keep an eye on the red-orange corks bobbing in the water "Watch out for moccasins," she hollered. Shiny beetle bugs skated across the surface. A tiny black-and-yellow striped turtle boxed the water with its lizardlike feet and I tried to catch him, dipping the paper cup beneath his horny toes. He got away.

As I climbed over the mossy rocks to look for another

turtle, I heard Maisey start in on Mama about James's fishing pole. "Mama," she said, dangling her pole out over the water. She pointed to where James sat. "James's got that magic fishing pole and I want it."

I stepped onto a big rock so I could see them. James was pulling bream in as fast as his hook sank and the fish could take his bait. He must've been on a bed, but that didn't occur to Maisey.

"Swap with her, James," Mama sighed, narrowing her eyes. She stared out at the water where she'd just cast my line. Just like that, whatever Maisey wanted Maisey got, because she was eight; she was the baby and she could send Mama over the edge with her whining. Well, Mama made James swap with her and he did, but it didn't matter because he kept right on catching one silver fish after the other, shouting *"Bam!"* every time he caught one, then dropped it flopping in the grass. And Mama kept taking them off the hook for him, smoothing their fins, threading the nylon stringer through their gills, chuffing the fish down, then sinking the stringer back into the water.

I watched as she poked a gray worm on the hook for Maisey, because Maisey wouldn't touch a worm if her life depended on it. Maisey swung her line over the water. Even though I was too far away to see it, I knew how the worm touched the surface jerking and twitching, then disappeared, slowly sinking.

I was thinking of the worm as I turned back around to look for more turtles, then I stepped on a slippery rock and my foot went out from under me. I whipped my arms around, grabbed at air, tried to keep myself from falling into that dark green moccasin-infested lake, but I was as jerky as that worm. I fell sideways into the water with a loud splash. The paper cup floated away.

As I sank, the water got cooler and spiky weeds wrapped round my legs like *a net of snakes!!* my mind screamed, and I kicked like crazy to get away from them. I shot to the surface, gulped air, imagined a tangle of moccasins writhing beneath me, and I panicked again. *I'm gonna drown I'm gonna drown I'm gonna drown.* Before I went under the second time, I heard James call my name, "Lily," and opened my eyes wide, screaming *Help*, but the word gurgled back down my throat with fishy-tasting water and I sank again, eyes open to a blur of green, my legs and arms wheeling madly. Mama couldn't save me no matter how much she loved water; she couldn't even swim herself.

When I bobbed up again, Mama stood on the dock, staring at me as if I were the cork on her fishing line. I fought to keep my head above the surface. The water tasted like the silver bodies of fish. Mama was solving a problem in her head: *Should I have used crickets or worms? Three minus one is two. Fish or cut bait.* James screamed again, his voice echoing across the canal, "Mama, save her! Mama!" Maisey just stood there with a pole in her hand.

Mama didn't move. I struggled to keep afloat, beat the water with my hands. She was going to let me drown and was weighing her gains against her losses. Watching me, eyes flat as pennies. I was Not the Right Kind of Girl. Never had been. Panicked, I went under again, holding my breath, my chest about to burst. I sank even though I kicked hard against the water.

Then there was an explosion, a blur of bubbles. Mama jumped into the lake next to me and sank beneath the surface, facing me, her eyes wide open. Her skin was waxy-looking underwater, like the worm on Maisey's hook. She held her hands out to me, scissored her legs. Her red hair floated above her head like silky grass. Silver bubbles leaked out of her mouth and nose. She clutched my hands and we sank deeper, where there was no sound. The water grew dark green in my mouth, the color of trees when night is falling. Her face was a question mark. That was the last I saw of her before everything went black. I floated backward through space, twitching like Maisey's worm, sinking, a voice whirling through my head, *Wish I'd never had you.*

Back in time, Wizard of Oz style. Armless. Legless. A fish. A rocking chair. Mama's lap. Her voice, low and whispery, warm against my ear *Blue, blue Lily. When you slid out of me, your skin was so blue and silvery, I thought you were a fish.*

Or a boy or a boy or a boy or a boy or a boy or a boy

When I opened my eyes again, I was sprawled out flat on my back in the damp and spiky grass, Mama bent over me, grunting like an animal, pushing her hands hard against my chest, her red hair wet and hanging ropy down the sides of her face, her dark eyes wild and furious. Clouds wheeled across the blue sky behind her head. A flock of blackbirds. Maisey crying. James kneeling in the grass, chanting, "Is she gonna die, is she gonna die, is she gonna die?" Drops of water fell onto my face as Mama rocked back and forth, huh, huh, huh, banging the hell out of my ribs, and I thought *She's not gonna stop till she kills me.* Then I rolled over onto my side and threw up.

I curled into a ball in the grass, thinking, *She let me drown.*

I knew I was right. She'd stopped on the end of the dock, eyed me as if I were a cork bobbing in the water. If she'd waited any longer I would've drowned, and it would've looked like an accident. She could drown us all and no one would know the difference. But I knew I could've drowned her too, could've pulled her to the bottom of the canal.

After I threw up, I watched the blue sky like a movie screen, pictured Mama sinking into the murky green water, her hair waving above her head like seaweed, her face tilted up, eyes and mouth open, her arms stretched toward me as I pushed her under. She sank slowly, and I treaded water and watched until she sank so deeply that I couldn't see her anymore and the water closed over her, the surface still and blank. Water could solve all of our problems.

Nobody said a word about what happened. My drowning was over before I even shook the water out of my hair. My family always left the scene of the accident. We burned rubber.

The water smoothed out, the surface unrippled, as if nothing had happened.

I waited for Mama to punch me in the nose for making her jump in the water like that, but she didn't even yell at me. She didn't yell at any of us. She wouldn't look at us either. She gathered the poles together, balanced them on her shoulder, and carried them to the car.

We followed her. James lay the fish on some newspapers on the floor by the backseat, where they panted softly, their eyes shiny as dimes, their fins fanned out like sails. Then he climbed up front with Mama, smiling now, his face still streaked with tears. "I didn't think you were going to save her," he said in a high voice that sounded like a question.

We all wanted her to reassure us that of course she was going to save me. But she didn't say anything. She pushed her hair back and narrowed her eyes at the windshield like she was trying to see something far, far away. Me and Maisey climbed into the backseat, Maisey scootching close to the window to get away from my wet clothes.

The fish writhed in a pile beneath my feet. We had a stringer full. They smelled green like the lake. Dribbles of dark red blood ran onto the floor from where the hooks had torn their mouths. They breathed softly, some arching their ribbed tail fins. All those eyes, those cloudy blobs of jelly, were on me; now I knew how horrible it must be for them, fish out of water, breathing the hard dry air that blew in the back window.

When we got home, Mama went in the house to change. Still dripping wet, I carried the stringer of fish around to the backyard where Daddy would come out and gut and scale them beneath the pecan tree. Careful not to let the fish fin me, I slid their rigid bodies off the stringer one at a time—I couldn't stand the chuffing sound of the nylon rubbing against their mouths. I dropped them into a bucket full of water, my hands sticky with blood and fish slime. Some of them bloomed alive again in the bloody water, arced their bodies, swam in a circle not much bigger than they were.

Daddy walked across the yard with his knife, sat in his chair next to the bucket, spread some newspapers onto the ground. "What happened to you?" he asked, not waiting for an answer. "Got a stringer full," he said. "That's some fishing."

"James was on a bed," I said, dipping my hands into the water to rinse them.

Mama came outside. Her hair was still damp but she didn't seem to care. She lay in the grass in dappled shade beneath the pecan tree, next to the fish bucket. Daddy scooped up a fish, began scraping the scales off with his knife. They fell into a pile like flakes of wet snow.

"Dwayne Edwards," she sighed, "you will not believe what happened today."

Daddy was way past not believing anything Mama said or did. He finished scraping the fish, cut its head off, dropped the head onto the paper. Its eyes were foggy now. Then, with one more movement, he slit the fish's belly and dumped its shiny purple guts out. Thick red blood oozed into the grass. He laid the gutted fish down.

Mama lifted one arm toward the sky. "I almost drowned today saving Lily," she said. And even though I knew that wasn't true—I was the one who drowned, really drowned—I didn't say anything. I'd heard enough about how me and my brother and sister had kept her from her real life, the one with the convertible Cadillac, the wind and the pink flamingos, to know that saving me was a form of drowning for her.

Daddy nodded, glancing at me with a look that said he'd heard those words a thousand times before: *I almost drowned, almost drowned, almost drowned.* He hummed a George Jones tune under his breath, his hands strumming a fish with the knife, as Mama described jumping in the lake, fighting to pull me to safety. I sat in the prickly grass and listened to the rise and fall of her voice, the scratchy sound of Daddy's knife scraping the fish. Flecks of silvery fishscale sparkled against Daddy's skin, the hairs on his arm.

That night when I crawled into bed next to Maisey, she slid away from me as if I were the Creature from the Black

Lagoon. Mama glided in to tell us good night. When she leaned over me to kiss Maisey, I smelled the sweet almond scent of Jergens lotion. Then she grasped my hand and looked deep into my eyes and whispered so I could barely hear the words, "You need to be more careful."

When she left the room, I lay still, wondering what she'd meant. I'd seen a movie where a man in a dark suit held a gun next to some poor guy's head, muttering the words, "You gotta be more careful," and I didn't think she meant it that way, but I wasn't sure.

I fell asleep and dreamed I tumbled into a pool of black water surrounded by cypress trees bearded with Spanish moss. I sank like a stone. Then the water smoothed out, shimmery and still as a mirror. Mama leaned over and smiled at her reflection.

2

Daddy was as crazy as Mama. He didn't climb trees or try to drown us, but he had a way of not hearing or seeing things, just like those monkeys who clap their hands over their ears and eyes. Maybe it was because he was the baby in his family, which was hard to picture because he was baldheaded and had hairy titties. His father died when Daddy was only six months old. James asked how and Daddy said during a flu epidemic that swept through Georgia like a flood. But that was hard to picture, too, because all of us had had the flu at least once and none of us had died.

The summer before my drowning, Daddy and I stood in the graveyard at the Hebron church in Withlacoochee, Georgia, during a family reunion. Hundred-year-old oak trees made a sighing sound whenever the wind blew. I kicked my shoes off and walked in the bone-white sand surrounding the graves. Weathered conch shells as big as my head were propped against crumbling gray tombstones. Daddy's oldest sister, Maylene, screwed up her old wrinkled face at me when I said something about the flu epidemic that killed their father.

"Papa didn't die from the flu, honey," she said. "After your daddy was born, Papa took his shotgun, walked down to the Withlacoochee River, sat in the shade beneath a willow tree, and shot himself in the head."

Daddy looked up for a minute and I watched for his reaction. I pictured his Papa's blood running down the grassy bank into the muddy river, fish nipping at the surface to get at his splattered brains. Daddy took a deep drag off his cigarette and turned away, staring off into the distance, his head shrouded in the haze of blue smoke drifting out of his mouth, his eyes squinched up. Fading himself out. He never did set the story straight. Never. It was like we'd never gone to that graveyard. He kept on pretending his daddy died from the flu. I pretended, too. But I knew. And he knew I knew.

. . . . .

The day after I drowned, Mama crawled into bed and burrowed under the covers like a mole—to protect herself against coming down with pneumonia, she said. I didn't see how jumping into a lake was any different than taking a bath. But climbing into bed was her favorite way of dealing with trouble of most any kind, so Daddy took me and Maisey on a long drive in the Fairlane, to get us away from her. James had already tramped into the cagelike shadows of the bamboo jungle across the street where he played soldier by himself, like he always did, shooting his own thin body dead, over and over.

As we rolled down the street past a tangle of purple wisteria, I wanted to ask Daddy how it felt to have a father who shot himself in the head, thinking maybe he could offer some advice on living with a woman who tried to drown me, but I didn't want to hurt his feelings. His daddy killed himself, and he'd made up his own story about what had happened. I guess I'd have to make up my own story, too.

We crossed Mosquito Creek where tea-colored water flowed beneath a cluster of scrub oaks, and passed the black folks' Laundromat on our way to River Junction where a train was rolling through. But the train whistled once loudly then stopped dead in its tracks out in front of Parkman's. At Easter, you could buy blue-and-pink dyed biddies from old man Parkman, then hold their tiny bodies in your hand for a week before they died and grew stiff as rabbits' feet.

Daddy cut the engine off and we sat in the car and stared out the window at heat shimmering in waves off Southern Cross and Santa Fe boxcars. The car filled with the smell of melting tar.

Maisey started to whine about how hot it was. She could work herself into a fit to where she'd get mad at Daddy for the sun shining. She was on her way to some real blubbering, chant-moaning, "I'm hot, Daddy, I'm so hot. I'm hothothothothot." Her brown hair was plastered in strings to the sides of her face, and she bounced up and down. I sweated in the backseat watching her, grateful we weren't with Mama. This was the kind of thing that would make Mama want to drown us both. But Daddy knew what to do.

He glanced over at Maisey. "Did I ever tell you the story about the woman who couldn't wait?"

I leaned forward. Stared at the black fringe of hair that cupped Daddy's shiny head like a U. He was going to tell us a story about Mama. The woman who couldn't wait to get rid of her children.

Maisey wiped her nose and stopped moaning. "No."

"Well," Daddy said. "She'd just walked out of Parkman's with a big brown sack of groceries and was on her way home to Happy Town when the train chugged through and stopped. Sweat ran down the sides of her face, dripped salty into her eyes. Her shirt was soaked. She got tired standing in the boiling sun next to an L&N boxcar, shifting her groceries from one arm to the next, and decided to crawl into the shadows beneath the train, to get to the other side."

Maisey tilted toward the windshield to look out at the boxcars, murmuring under her breath, "She crawled under a train?"

"Yes," Daddy said. "She drug her sack of groceries behind her. Her legs stuck out in the sun," dusty with dirt. All of a sudden there was a loud metal sound, a banging noise, the sharp screech of wheels moving from a total stop. The woman couldn't move fast enough," Daddy said. "Her grocery bag tore open, and three small oranges rolled out into the sun. Before the woman could move, the train chugged right over her, chopping her legs clean off."

"OOOOOhhhh," moaned Maisey, squeezing her eyes closed.

Daddy nodded, his lips pressed shut in a straight line.

Jesus, I thought. I looked out the window at the road beside the tracks. I could see those legs. Chopped off like fish heads. Lying there. Bloody. With shoes on. What was it like to pick them up? One in each hand. Did they twitch like broken-off lizard tails?

I wondered if Mama had ever thought of shoving us under a train. Or maybe even crawling under a train herself. Sometimes people jumped in front of trains when they couldn't stand things anymore.

Maisey hung big-eyed out the car window, looking for bloodstains near the tracks. Daddy said he didn't know what happened to the woman, or where she was now, but Maisey better get her ass back inside the car or she would end up like the man with one arm. The train jerked into motion and Daddy cranked the car. We never did find out where the woman was or who picked up the woman's legs or what they did with them. I imagined her sitting in shade on a porch somewhere in Happy Town, pink and brown scarred-up stumps sticking out from under her blue dress like sausages. That was just like Daddy to tell a stupid story with no ending to it.

We rumbled over the tracks, drove on out past Happy Town, where most of the black people lived, past cow fields studded with twisted pine trees, past the Lost in Space jook joint, to Hardaway. When we got to Renfroe's Country Store, Daddy bought us blue raspberry Icees and a paper sack full of jawbreakers and firecracker bubblegum. When he handed me the sack of candy it was easy to imagine him as the baby of his family, even if he was baldheaded, and I felt sorry for him all over again for him losing his daddy so soon after he was born.

When we got home that evening, Mama was still in bed, sleeping. Dreaming her way south to Monkey Jungle and Cypress Gardens, I guessed. After checking on her, Daddy settled onto the concrete steps in front of our house, rumpled up in khakis, arms and legs folded, bare feet shimmed into black wingtips too scuffed up for Sunday, a cigarette poking from his lip. Even though there was nowhere to look, unless you counted the Matthiesens' yard, he looked off into the distance, past a fence dripping with honeysuckle, through a stand of pines, toward River Junction. I sat next to him but got the feeling he blocked me out of his sight.

"Mama let me drown," I said. "She stood on the dock and watched me go under about twenty times. I passed out."

I looked at his face to see if he was shocked.

He wasn't.

He sucked on his cigarette, exhaled the words with puffs of blue smoke. "Honey, if you drowned, you wouldn't be here. I think your mama saved your life." He looked at the hot orange end of his cigarette. "She said you put up a helluva fight."

I considered his words. Maybe I was wrong. All I could think of was the look Mama had on her face when she grabbed my hands, like she wasn't sure she wanted to save me. That and how we sank together, down into the dark green water. Daddy took another drag, sucked the blue smoke in deep, his eyes slitted, then let the smoke drift past his thin lips like a ribbon. He didn't thump the ash, just held the cigarette between thick, fat fingers and let the ash grow till it crumpled into itself and fell.

When he went into the house, he sat in his chair at the kitchen table next to a saucer full of butts. Mama had gotten out of bed. Now she sat coiled on one end of the black Naugahyde couch, feet beneath her, biting copper-colored bobby pins in her mouth like fangs, rolling her hair onto pink foam curlers, spraying till both the curl and the air dripped with so much White Rain I could taste its sweet chemical smell. Maybe the White Rain did something to her. As she pinned her hair to the curlers, she stared off into space like she was thinking something important.

James begged Daddy to smoke a whole cigarette without dropping the ash, and he did, sucking deep and hard, the tip glowing orange, hot and bright as a flare, the white ash growing, bending, Daddy not looking at us but at the wall, like he could see right through it. Just then a train whistled in the distance and I heard the faint rumble of boxcars as I watched Daddy vanish in a cloud of blue smoke. I knew our Daddy was an artist; he was the original disappearing man.

3

My family fit right in at Chattahoochee where there were more crazy people than sane ones. In 1958, the year I was born, Daddy said there were seven thousand patients in the hospital, almost twice the number of people living in our town. Together, they made Chattahoochee the biggest city in Gadsden County, except that Chattahoochee itself wasn't a real city. It was a trap, like one of those man-eating plants. Whenever I rode into town from the east in the backseat of Daddy's Fairlane, I looked over his shoulder and saw tall buildings clustered together in the distance like Someplace Else. I pretended we were about to enter the Emerald City of Oz. We'd drive right up to the wizard and I'd ask him to please, please, please let me be a boy so I could marry Rae Miller and fly out of this made-up town with her, and Daddy would ask for courage, because I thought that might be what was wrong with him. But when we passed the blue Lions Club welcome sign there was no more make-believe. I was still a girl and Daddy still needed courage. The tall city buildings didn't belong to Someplace Else; they belonged to crazy people. Seven-story buildings air conditioner cool with elevators and generators, and giant fans. Most were white-painted brick; some even had gingerbread trim and huge wraparound porches.

At the hospital, there was a sewage treatment plant, a water tower, a red-brick smokestack taller than any building within thirty miles, a fire station, a police force, and a baseball diamond right next to the laundry where my grandmother had worked washing the patients' sheets and clothes before she died. The field where we had our Halloween carnival belonged to the patients, and some of them came, too; mostly chain-smoking men with nervous yellow hands who walked over the damp grass to play Go Fish and Pickpocket. For a dime, children could ride screaming through the hospital grounds on the back of an antique fire truck, their arms waving above their heads, their warm bodies lurching together in a knot as the fire chief swung around curves, driving like a maniac, trying his best to scare everyone. Even the fire truck belonged to the patients.

Across the grounds, at the hospital, the patients had an auditorium where they went to watch scratched-up Westerns or listen to the high-school band mangle some music. They even had a playground with chin-up bars and a swing, although the only person who ever used the swing was a patient named Zack Bell, a curly-haired man who swung for hours at a time, his head bowed, his eyes closed, his hands folded in his lap. Kids at school said his brain had been eaten up by syphilis. Mama had hushed me when I asked her what syphilis was.

The hospital was the city, more of a city than Chattahoochee ever was. If you mentioned Chattahoochee, most people thought you were talking about the hospital anyway. They didn't even know there was a town. There wouldn't have been one if it weren't for the hospital. Chattahoochee was stubby, strung down Washington Street like a row of dusty shoe boxes between two traffic lights. Nichol's Flower Shop and the field where we had our carnival sat on one end, and the Riverview Bait and Tackle and Galloway's Restaurant sat on the other. Everything from the Jitney Jungle to Chattaburger was clumped in between like some toy town a kid threw together.

Downtown Chattahoochee was small, but it made me feel smaller, squashed, especially when I rode my bike over weeds springing from the cracked sidewalk. I knew I didn't belong on those narrow streets, couldn't make myself fit between the lines. At least some of the patients got to leave; they wouldn't memorize the cracks in the gray sidewalk, wouldn't remember where the clumps of dandelions grew. They wouldn't stand in front of the plate-glass window of Nichol's Flower Shop, staring past their reflections at buckets of carnations, chrysanthemums, and roses, the only kinds of flowers you could get in a small town. They wouldn't wonder, *Where are the birds of paradise? Where are the blue orchids?*

They would never stand in the dim oily-smelling shoe fix-it shop with Mr. Gleason, a man with thin white hair, hands creased and blackened with grease, a wooden leg darkened to the color of tea. They would never see the piles and piles of stiff and curling leather shoes people dropped off but never picked up. Like they knew they weren't going anywhere, shoes or not.

They wouldn't memorize the porches on the fronts of wooden houses, or wonder who was sitting in the shadows behind the gray screens, or imagine what the shadows said to each other, or what they would've said if they knew how things really were, the way I did. I imagined the whole town murmuring as I walked down the street, *She's got a nutty mother; her father can't pay the bills; she acts like a boy.* But that wasn't the half of it.

We might as well have been a circus act as far as our neighbors went. I figured they could hear Mama yelling bloody murder at us all the time, and I didn't want to have anything to do with them. I never had kids over to my house, especially not Rae Miller—Mama didn't want me anywhere near her because she was white trash. She wanted me to be friends with this girl named Brenda Thomas. I never did invite Brenda over, even though Mama liked her. Brenda was the Right Kind of Girl, Mama said, meaning her daddy was a big shot at the hospital, but I don't think Mama noticed that none of us ever had kids over, especially not the right kind. Couldn't she see James marching across the front yard, alone, carrying a garbage can lid for a shield, shooting imaginary soldiers, then turning the gun on himself? Couldn't she see how Maisey cowered when she screamed, "I wish I'd never had you?"

I'd seen enough when I went behind Brenda's doors one time to know that Mama wasn't the right kind of mama. Brenda's living room was a shag-carpeted museum of Brenda. The walls were plastered with hand-tinted photographs of Brenda as a baby, as a toddler, as a first-grader. Mrs. Thomas bronzed Brenda's baby shoes herself, then used them to decorate a lamp. She recorded the first five years of Brenda's life in one of those memory books—actually writing down important dates: first step, first word, first tooth. She did things right. She even had one of those Kool-Aid pitchers you order off the pack of Kool-Aid, along with the matching cups.

I knew Mama couldn't compete—she bought three of those memory books, one each for me, James, and Maisey, filled in the parts about how long we were and how much we weighed at birth, then stopped. She threw them in the trash one day when she was cleaning out the closets. That I could live with, but I didn't want my friends to find out that she could cuss a blue streak, or that she'd climb a tall tree to get away from us. I didn't want them to find out that she didn't love me in the same easy way their mothers loved them, that she'd let me drown. She did let me drown.

She sure didn't bronze our baby shoes. I mean, she loved us, but she didn't like us all the time. Especially me. And she wasn't afraid to say so. Not even with an audience. That was the kind of house I lived in. No one could come in.

Sometimes, I rode my bike all over town to get away from the bad weather Mama brought into our house. But after my drowning, the water-colored sky came down anyway, hovered right over Washington Street, flattened me into the blue-gray pavement, pressed the air right out of my body. If I took thirty seconds and pedaled all the way through town past Galloway's and the bait shop, I could look off into the smoky distance and see the tops of oaks and pines lining the banks of the Apalachicola River. They looked like hills, gray in the distance, then gray-blue the closer they got, then blue. Right before the bridge, the road dropped off into a jungle of green. When I saw this green, I broke through all that water to the surface. I could breathe again. That green was the beginning of the Distance, the place I longed to go to, a place where the voices would disappear, where no one would know my name. A place I could breathe myself into being.

A person just driving through Chattahoochee, though, probably wouldn't feel drowned. They wouldn't be able to tell the difference between the townspeople and the patients, either. Sometimes it was hard even for me, especially with Mama straddling the line. I went to school with the daughter of one of the psychiatrists—the butcher at the Jitney Jungle caught him shoving plastic-wrapped steaks and pork chops down his pants. He wasn't any saner than Innertube. Mama said Innertube had been so wild when he came to the hospital that he'd been given a lobotomy to calm him down. Now he was a perfect angel.

I also knew Peanut, a tiny old man with black spots on his skin and eleven fingers who stood next to the brand-new silver garbage cans in front of the Western Auto and answered nine, no matter what you asked him. He wore a toy sheriff's badge on his pajama shirt and dipped Sweet Peach snuff. Even though I was only in the sixth grade by then, I was almost as tall as he was.

One Saturday, while Daddy picked up some bags of fertilizer, James and I cornered Peanut. We took turns asking him stupid questions so we could laugh at his one stupid answer. How many moons does Earth have? How many times have you kissed your sister? What's your mama's name? What town are you from? James looked around to see if Daddy was coming, and asked as quickly and softly as he could, "How many buttholes ya got?" And Peanut smiled and said, nine, nine, nine, nine, nine, flecks of brown snuff damp in the corners of his mouth, dotting his teeth. He wanted us to like him. Then he showed us his extra finger, holding out his blotchy hand, the tiny finger pointing right at us crookedly and James asked, "How many fingers ya got, Peanut?" for one more laugh.

The guys who lived in the hospital were *really* crazy. There were two kinds of crazy—the crazy we could live with and the crazy we couldn't live with. I wasn't always sure what the difference between them was.

4

Mama said she heard that Rae Miller's mother was nutty as a squirrel and I thought *Ha! talk about the pot calling the kettle black.* But her Mama *was* one of those you run and hide from. Just like mine. Right after the Millers moved to town, I spotted Mrs. Miller shuffling around the Dollar Store with her messed-up baby-doll hair, dragging her pink flip-flops over that dusty checkered floor, her dress stained with something brown. She was scary looking. It was hard to believe she was kin to Rae.

On the first day of sixth grade, I fell in love with Rae the minute I saw her because I could tell she was a girl like me. Not meant for the narrow streets of Chattahoochee. I saw her shadow first, stretched black like a stocking across the wooden floor of Mrs. Glisson's sixth-grade class. When I stepped into the room, there stood Rae next to a window, her face streaky as if she might have cried that morning, but later I found out it was just dirty. She wore an ugly beige vinyl coat, one button dangling from a thread. Her head glowed like a lamp, her hair was so white.

She acted like she was tuned in to a radio station, maybe

WOOF out of Dothan, Alabama; she swayed back and forth, kicked her scuffed-up go-go boots against the floor. Next to her, bent over the teacher's desk signing papers, hulked her big fat mama. Looking at them, I thought of how children love their ugly mothers no matter what. I always saw those mothers at the Halloween carnival—bucktoothed, crosseyed, or just plain ugly, standing in the grass next to the fishing booth, beautiful babies clamped onto their hips.

From the first day, Mama didn't want me to be friends with Rae because her father raked yards and her mother was a lunatic, a concern I thought odd coming from her.

Maisey chimed in, too, talking double time without even breathing, "Her daddy stinks like wet cigars and his eyes," she said, "you can't see the whites in them. Like Mr. B on *Hazel*," she said. "Remember when he played in that movie *The Man with the X-ray Eyes* and put that x-ray potion in his eyes so he could see naked women but how he ended up in a tent at a Holy Roller revival and the preacher screamed, 'If thine right eye offend thee, pluck it out,' and Mr. B. did because by then all he could see was skeletons? Her daddy's got eyes like that."

Mr. Miller was whip-thin and brown as snuff—I saw him pumping gas at the Tom Thumb—but x-ray eyes or not, by the end of the week Rae and I were best friends. We sprawled out on the orange clay hill at the playground and watched clouds skim across the sky while the other girls ran screaming from boys and pushed each other on swings. No one else wanted anything to do with us. When we got in line to go to the lunchroom, a couple of the girls made a show of looking at Rae's go-go boots, then giggled and whispered to each other. I didn't care. Rae and I were headed for bigger and better things than the school cafeteria.

She told me she lived in a shack on River Road and that she owned a horse named Blazer. Soon I was riding out there every day. I lied to Mama, told her I was going to play with Brenda, and she thought that was wonderful. I knew she'd never catch me because she'd rather die than talk to somebody normal like Brenda's mother. Mama never answered the telephone, and sometimes she hid in her bedroom when someone knocked on our door.

Rae and I rode Blazer round and round the shady backyard next to a field where Mr. Miller grew stalks of corn as tall as men.

"Watch my daddy walk my horse over me," Rae said one day. She leaned her head back and hollered *"Daddy!"* at the corn field. *"Daddy!"*

I heard a rustling, like paper bags rubbing together, like an animal rooting through the field, then Mr. Miller parted the thick green stalks and stepped into the yard. Rae handed him the reins without a word. She flopped down in the dark green grass beneath the limber branches of a mimosa tree and closed her eyes. She was so white and still she looked dead. Pink flowers delicate as hula skirts blew across the blades of grass. Mr. Miller tugged the worn leather reins and gently led Blazer one gray hoof after the other over Rae's body. I held my breath. A deerfly landed on Blazer's silky brown back and her whole skin twitched. She lifted her last hoof and placed it on the ground just past Rae's belly. I breathed again. I thought Rae was crazy—and her Daddy, too—for that.

When she got tired of letting the horse stroll over her, we went into the house for jelly jars of ice water. Rae's mother was watching wrestling on TV, slapping the naugahyde armrests with sweaty palms, hunched forward into the black-and-white TV, screaming, "Kill 'em, Dusty, kill 'em." Two half-naked men crab-walked around each other in the ring.

"They ain't for real," Rae said as we passed by, but her mama didn't hear her. Sweat slid down the sides of her puffy face. Rae looked over her shoulder at me and made the sign for "crazy," twirling her finger in a circle by her ear. I followed her into the kitchen and stood next to the sink while she dumped ice into our glasses, waiting for the rusty water to run out of the pipes before filling them. A pot of greens simmered on the stove.

"Mama's a Holy Roller," Rae whispered. "Sometimes she gets so excited watching Dusty Rhodes pound the crap out of somebody, she catches the spirit."

"What?" I said. I didn't know what "catching the spirit" meant.

"She'll get the spirit, start speaking in tongues, a language nobody understands. Sounds like baby talk." Rae handed me the glass of water. "She calls herself an open vessel—I call her a cracked pot." She screwed her face up at me.

We marched into Rae's room with our ice water and piled onto her high bed. I dropped a scratched-up single onto Rae's ratty record player and watched as she held an empty Coke bottle to her lips and sang every word to "Band of Gold," twisting her hips and jabbing at the air with her hands.

The record ended. I looked around Rae's room. The dirty white walls were plastered with blue and gold ribbons. Silver trophies stood lined up on her dresser. Horse stuff. She'd won prizes galloping around dusty corrals on top of

Blazer. Barrel-racing in clouds of brown dirt. I'd never won anything. Still, I wanted to impress her. She thought *her* mother was crazy.

"I got something you won't believe," I said.

"What?" she asked. "A go-cart?"

"No," I said. "Something happened to me last summer. I died." I'd never said those words before, and I wondered if they were really true. Had I actually been dead? I didn't know. People said you'd see a light. I didn't. I sank deep into the water. And everything went black. I turned into a fish, though. I felt okay now.

Rae cocked her eyebrows at me, her eyes wide.

"My mama drowned me," I said. After I talked to Daddy, I believed my drowning might've been an accident, but that only lasted a little while. My falling into the lake might've been an accident, but Mama standing there watching me go under wasn't.

"Whaddaya mean," Rae asked. "She really drowned you?"

"Well, we were fishing and I fell in the lake and sank and she stood on the dock and watched me go under until I passed out and was dead. Ain't that drowning?"

"You were really dead? Hell," Rae said. "Why didn't you call the police? She oughta be put away for that. My mama wouldn't even do that to me. Here. Look at these," she said, handing me a pair of black patent-leather shoes. "My cousin gave them to me. They got taps on them. Why'd she drown you?" she asked.

I turned the shoes over. They were cracked and coated with dust. Silver crescents of metal were nailed to the scuffed-up heels. "She wanted to be Miss Florida and ride around in a Cadillac convertible, but she got kids instead." I handed the shoes back to Rae, even though I wanted to dust them off and keep them. I felt like they had special powers. Like Dorothy's ruby slippers.

"How'd you get undrowned?" she asked.

"She pulled me out of the water and beat on me till I threw up."

"Sounds like she drowned you, then saved you. Hell, she might be Jesus," Rae said, then burst into laughter. "For God's sake don't tell Mama that story; she'll think your mama's Jesus come again. Raising the dead." She sang loudly: "I once was lost but now am found, I thought I was swimming but I really drowned." She howled again and I had to laugh with her, even though I thought God might strike her dead for talking that way. Then she dropped another record on and we took turns clacking away at the wood floor with those tap shoes.

5

Our house floated on a lake. That's what it seemed like that Saturday. There wasn't any riding the bike out to Rae's. I watched as rain streamed down the windows, blurred the trees and bushes, puddled the yard. Wondered what Rae was doing. Imagined her looking out her own window, wondering about me.

Any minute the house would break loose from its foundation, drift downriver. I'd be the pilot, and Mama'd finally get to see a little bit of Florida—in style, too. I'd drape a lime-green scarf around her neck and we'd float down the Apalachicola River toward the Gulf of Mexico in the houseboat to end all houseboats. She'd be in such a good mood that she wouldn't mind if we motored by River Road and picked Rae up.

But just then James blasted his trumpet in my ear and the house stopped being a boat and turned into one of those cartoon shanties where the walls heave and heave and heave, then explode with a giant *kapow*! James made another long farting sound with his horn, and Mama glanced up from washing the dishes with a weary-looking face that meant she'd be blowing her top soon, so I stole a bag of cookies when she stepped into her bedroom and signaled Maisey to follow me. We snuck out of the house.

Daddy's broke down Oldsmobile '98 sat rotting on flat tires in our front yard. A couple of years ago Mama and I were sitting at the red light uptown and she gave the old '98 gas, but we didn't move; the engine revved, but we didn't move, and it was because the transmission broke right there.

That day, Mama put the car in reverse and stepped on the gas slowly and the car moved and it was funny. The car wouldn't go forward, only backward, so she said, "I guess that's that, I'll have to drive it on back to the house," and she threw her arm over the seat and started backing to the house, backing, and we laughed the whole way. She didn't even get mad, and I loved her for that because our stuff was always breaking but she laughed and said, "How'd you like to drive to Philadelphia like this?"

People drove up behind us, our cars eye to eye, and we waved at them as if we were in a parade or something, driving along in one of those trick cars. Mama backed the car up our driveway, pulled it into the grass and cut the engine off. And there it sat.

At first Daddy acted like he knew how to fix it; he lifted the hood and poked at some greasy wires with a stick. Then he checked the oil and slammed the hood shut. Finally, he just mowed around it. I washed it sometimes so it wouldn't look so bad, so it'd look like we were going to get it fixed one day, but I knew we weren't. Once something broke at our house, it stayed broke.

For a while, me, Maisey, and James all played in the car. We took turns driving. We pretended to go to the Alligator

Farm and Marineland, places Mama'd dreamed of going before she had us. She'd gotten brochures for one of James's geography projects on Florida, thumbed through all the glossy pages, holding up pictures to show us what we'd made her miss: an Indian wrestling an alligator, an orange cockatoo riding a tricycle, a mermaid. "People from all over the country come to Florida to see these things," she said. "I live right here and I'll never see a one of them."

I wanted her to sit in the car with us, just once, to show her we could go anywhere we wanted. But she wouldn't. She just didn't know how to pretend. Neither did James when it came to the car. After a few weeks, he got bored and went back to shooting himself over and over in the front yard. Then the car belonged to Maisey and me.

Lightning shot across the dark, gray sky as Maisey and I ran to the Olds. We got drenched. Sheets of rain beat the roof and blurred the windows so the car became the Scenic Submarine. It was my turn to drive first, so I headed south to Silver Springs to see the wild monkeys and watch Ross Allen milk a rattlesnake and then drove over to Monkeytown U.S.A. to look at the giant mankiller clam. I wanted Rae to be with me; the car was as good as her horse, even if it did smell moldy from being closed up.

Maisey wanted to drive us to Rainbow Springs. The brochure said we would be "transported into a strange but delightful underwater world on the Scenic Submarine Boat Trip," that we'd see giant leopard gar, monster black bass, and ghostly blue shad swim past the porthole. As Maisey drove, she lifted her hand like a tour guide, pointing out the windows of the car, careful, though, to keep her eyes on the road. She deepened her voice and drew out her words, trying not to laugh, "And if you look to your left, you will see the only giant black bass left in the whole wide world." We set the trip meter and drove and drove.

After a while, we stretched out on the blue vinyl seats and read *Little Lotta* comic books and munched on Chips Ahoy and waited for the leopard gar and the giant black bass to appear, their shadowy figures rippling darkly beyond the fogged-over windows. But the shadow that appeared didn't belong to the giant black bass; it belonged to Mama. She hunkered outside the car in the pouring-down rain, hollering at first, then banging on the windows. We could barely hear her muffled voice over the roar of the rain: "Y'all are in big trouble. Now get out of that car."

Maisey had locked the doors and she wasn't going to unlock them now. We crouched together in the backseat. Surely Mama would go back into the house. Get out of the rain. But she didn't. She darted to the other side of the car and began kicking the door. Wham wham wham. A bright flash of lightning whitened her dark face. Wet hair drooped in points over her eyes. From the way she looked, I knew we'd better do something or we were dead, and I was about to open the door farthest away from her and scream, "Let's run," but then the kicking stopped and Mama was nowhere to be seen. I figured she must've gone inside. I stepped outside of the car. It was still raining hard, pricking my eyes, running off the end of my nose. Thunder rumbled in the distance. The sky had disappeared.

Then I saw her. A blurry figure at the bottom of our driveway. She faced the road, looked like she was waiting for a light to change. Then, as if the light had changed, she stepped out into the street and began walking toward Happy

Town. Maisey and I stood in the yard and watched as she shrank away in the distance, swallowed by the falling rain. I imagined her drowning in all that water.

We ran into the house and dried off with towels. Then we plopped down on the bed in our room, waiting. The room smelled of airplane glue; James must've been putting one of his stupid war planes together. Every now and then Maisey or I would look out the window toward the street. Mama might be crossing the bridge at Mosquito Creek by now, the red water gushing beneath her. Or she might be getting close to that old brokedown church where somebody said they sacrificed goats and threw the bloody bones into the woods. I never could ride my bike anywhere near that spot and wondered if Mama had the nerve to walk right past it.

The sky was a gray smudge. I wondered if Mama was ever going to come back, or if she'd just keep on walking south till she hit the gates of Monkeytown. She knew a woman patient who walked away from the hospital, made it all the way to a grocery store in Dothan, Alabama, before somebody found her trying to set fire to a pyramid of toilet paper and brought her back. I wondered if someone would see Mama walking in the rain near the brokedown church and think she'd gone nuts. Maisey must've been thinking the same thing. She turned away from the window and whispered, "Do you think they'll bring her back here or take her to the hospital?"

"She'll come back here by herself," I said. "She's an Aquarius. That's a water sign, Maisey, you know that."

Maisey gave me a look like she wanted to believe Mama would come back but wasn't sure.

I was right. Mama came back a couple of hours later, sopping wet but calm.

She walked into the kitchen and poured herself a glass of iced tea. Water dripped from her clothes onto the floor. Goose bumps prickled the skin on her arms. Maisey ran to get Mama a towel. "Where'd you go?" she asked, handing Mama the towel. "What'd you see?" as if Mama had gone on some kind of pleasure walk.

Mama sipped her tea. The towel she let fall to the floor.

"Did you go down to O'Dell's? Look," Maisey said, pointing at the kitchen counter where she'd tossed the wet bag of Chips Ahoy. "We put the cookies back."

Mama set her glass on the counter. "I couldn't find a deep enough ditch," she said, "so I decided to come home."

6

That soaking did Mama good. The next day she whistled "Raindrops Keep Falling on my Head," while she danced in front of the stove, cooking our breakfast. "I don't know what got into me yesterday," she said. She sat the plates in front of us. "I guess I couldn't bear the thought of my little girls sitting in a brokedown car going nowhere." She fluffed her hair up with her fingers the way she did sometimes before she came out with an announcement. "After breakfast," she said, "I'm gonna take y'all on a real adventure; I'm gonna show y'all how to make butterfly nets, then we're gonna go catch us some swallowtails."

Mama had a thing for delicate winged creatures, butterflies and moths. Not the brown ones though; she liked the fancy ones, like the pale green luna moth.

I already had a bug collection. Daddy had gotten me started the year before. He worked at Aubrey's Pest Control where he was an exterminator, but he liked bugs and so did I. He captured stag beetles, tiger beetles, giant water beetles, bugs so big they looked like windup toys.

Together, Daddy and I washed out Deep South mayonnaise

jars, Bama jelly jars. We stuffed them with green leaves, stabbed holes in the metal lids. I loved the velvety yellow and black fuzz of bumblebees, the glassy black bodies of beetles. I kept the bugs till they fell over dead, then pressed their crackly bodies into soft wads of cotton, framed them under glass like 3-D photographs, their shiny black legs still as sticks. Daddy thumbed through *Peterson's Guide to the Insects of North Florida*, reading out their Latin names: *Lucanus elephus, Euphoria fulgida.* I typed the names onto thin white paper I cut into strips and pasted beneath the insects' bodies.

Mama thought I was cruel.

But she was in such a good mood that day, the whole house seemed charged with magic. The only thing missing was Rae. She would've loved hunting butterflies, but I was sure she down at the Assembly of God with her mother. Mama dug through the hall closet until she found the leftover bolt of pink tulle she'd used to make my fairy costume when I was in the second grade and that she'd made Easter chicks and bunnies with later. She bent black metal coathangers into haloes, threaded needles, and showed us how to sew the tulle into the shape of a net.

Then we were outside. In a field not far from home. Everything was perfect. Even the trees seemed greener after all that rain the day before. Mama was happy. Above us giant tiger swallowtails floated, then flickered yellow against the blue sky. We ran through grass, dandelions, pokeweed, heads up, eyes open. Set loose by the crush of our feet, feathery seeds zipped up and away. Ahead of us, grasshoppers green as crayons leapt high, skimming air. We ran in the wind, chasing butterflies, cloudless sulphurs, zebra swallowtails, trying to catch them without hurting them. Mama wanted us to let them go after we looked at them.

Maisey caught a red admiral. We gathered around her as Mama reached into the net and carefully grasped the butterfly by the thorax, holding it out for us to see. "Ohhhh," she said. "Its wings are just like a painting. See. Just look," she said softly, holding a magnifying glass over the butterfly's wings as they opened and closed slowly. Tiny specks of blue and red dotted the wings like fish scales. "Look how pretty they are. Just look and then let them go. See?" She flicked her hand and the butterfly flew away.

Maisey and James were good about letting their butterflies go. But I wasn't. Suddenly, the butterflies were more important to me than Mama's good mood. I had a tiger swallowtail, a giant swallowtail, a zebra, and a painted lady, and I didn't want to look at them and let them go. I wanted to keep them. Their blues and reds and yellows and blacks. And that ruined everything.

Mama talked to my back on the way home. "You weren't supposed to keep them," she said. I glanced over my shoulder at her. Her eyes were filmy with tears. I thought she was nicer to those butterflies than she'd ever been to us, and I knew she was faking those tears to make me feel bad. I walked faster, holding my net tight, in case she tried to grab it from me. Every now and then I lifted it to have a look. The butterflies were gathered at the bottom, folded up tight like paper hearts.

Maisey stood in the kitchen, glaring at me, and Mama wept at the table, saying she'd never take me butterfly hunting again. Daddy ignored her and showed me how to put the butterflies to sleep right away, the mason jars, the balls of puffy white cotton soaked in chloroform. Innocent stuff. "This is what they use to put patients to sleep for operations," Daddy said, and I remembered the time I had my tonsils out and the doctor clapped a mask over my face and told me to count back from one hundred, and I closed my eyes and counted and saw Day-Glo skeletons driving go-carts around a deep black pit and then I passed out.

I thought of these things vaguely as I placed my butterflies into the glass jar with the poisonous cotton ball, Mama weeping quietly in the background. I didn't feel bad about making her cry. I wanted her to cry. The butterflies fluttered against my jar, beating their wings madly at first, then more slowly, then not at all, and I felt like I was getting back at her.

When the butterflies slept, when they slept so deeply they wouldn't feel it, I pulled them out of the jar, spread their delicate, papery wings, and stuck pins through their velvety bodies, my fingertips dusted with color. Then I framed them in Hav-A-Tampa cigar boxes still fragrant with tobacco.

7

"*I got something* to show you," Rae said one afternoon. Her breath turned to fog in the cold air. The leaves had fallen off the trees by then and the gray branches were naked. We climbed on our bikes and pedaled down the dirt road. I was riding Maisey's old tore-up bicycle, and the rusty chain kept falling off. When I stopped to fix it, a flock of geese flew over in a giant V, their shadows flitting across the orange road. I rubbed my fingers against my pants to warm them. My fingertips smelled like metal.

We rolled up to a wooden shack so brokedown it slanted to one side. One of the windows was busted open, and gray strands of spiderwebs feathered back and forth in the breeze like wisps of smoke.

We walked up the crooked steps and went inside. Mouse turds, yellowed scraps of newspaper, and broken bits of glass were scattered across the dusty floor. The air was filled with the moldering smell of something long dead—a mouse? A possum? The rotting house? Left abandoned.

"Whaddaya think?" she asked.

"It stinks," I said.

"Hell, we'll get used to it," she said. "Then we won't even notice."

And she was right; the truth was a human being could get used to anything, and we did get used to the smell after a while, or maybe our being there drove it out.

Rae and I cleaned the house as best we could. We brought in stuff to make it more homey: comic books, a transistor radio, my bug collection, Rae's horse ribbons. Rae even brought in an old rug for the floor.

I got real good at telling Mama lies: I was staying after school to help the teachers; I was joining the school choir; I was working on a science project in the library. I think she was glad I was gone—one less body hanging around the house for her to get mad at.

One day, after we'd been going to the house for a while, Rae showed up with a peanut-butter jar full of milk and a bag of cookies. She sat the jar of milk on the table. "Let's pretend we're going to outer space," she said, and she scooped a handful of leaves that had blown in through a broken window, shredded them into powder and threw it up in the air. Being with her was like being with a boy in a way. She wasn't afraid of anything. She stole figs and pecans from her neighbors' trees, smoked homemade cigarettes and wasn't scared to walk past the falling-down church where people said the men sacrificed goats and tossed the bloody bones out back. She poked around in the woods looking for the bones, said there weren't any. Still, bones or not, she was fearless.

Mama didn't want me to be anywhere near Rae, and if she'd known I was alone in a shack with her, it would have been almost as bad as if I'd been with a boy. Maybe worse.

Knowing that gave me a queasy and delicious feeling,

the same feeling I felt the first time I sucked on one of Rae's homemade cigarettes. That day I almost got caught. When I walked past Mama, she pulled me close and sniffed my hair. "You been burning something?" she asked. And I lied, told her old Mr. Benefield was burning leaves in his yard and that I stood on the sidewalk in a cloud of blue smoke to watch. She let my arm go, and I saw that she believed me, and I knew that she really didn't have a choice because she spent half her life in bed, and when she wasn't in bed she was at work, and when she wasn't at work she was with us. After my drowning, I'd seen how easy it was to make up stories about what happened. You just tell yourself something.

Rae opened the jar of milk and passed it to me along with the bag of cookies. "I dare you to take your clothes off and run outside." She munched on a cookie, tapped her foot. "I bet you won't do it," she said.

She pulled her clothes off easily, just ripped her shirt off over her head like any boy, then slid out of her pants, peeled off her underwear, left them in a pile at her feet. Her nakedness startled me. Her small breasts, her slim hips, her white skin. The way she stood there, waiting. A pale blue vein snaked across her belly.

From the time I was a little kid, Mama'd said you weren't supposed to be naked and you weren't supposed to look at naked people. Being naked was a sin. And a girl had so much to lose, Mama said. Her virginity's everything. It got to where I didn't even like seeing pregnant women 'cause I knew they'd done more than look.

Rae darted outside, leapt off the porch into the dried-up grass. With her bare feet she kicked at a pile of leaves, scattering them like ashes. I stood at the dirty window and watched as she turned cartwheels in front of the house. She was the only living thing in the world right then, naked beneath that gray tin sky. Her small breasts shifted under her skin. I felt like I was underwater, moving in slow motion, while Rae danced freely in the yard outside. She ran toward the window where I stood and shouted, "Come on! Nobody's going to see you. Don't be a damn sissy."

I couldn't stand being called a sissy. I looked around the room to make sure no one had sneaked in to see me, and slowly pulled my clothes off, dropping them to the floor. I shivered as goose bumps prickled over my body. When I opened the door and stepped outside, Rae shouted at me again, "Come on. Hurry up."

I jumped off the porch into the grass, my body stiff with cold. I couldn't move my arms and legs normally, but it was more than the cold. I felt like a skeleton must feel, stiff as bone out of a body, clacking like dried bamboo. Dizzy with cold and excitement.

Suddenly, Rae charged over to me, grabbed both my hands with hers and pulled me so close, our bodies brushed together in a band of heat. The smell of dried leaves rose between us.

"Pretend I'm Dean Fleming," she said, naming a handsome blond boy who was a senior. I wanted to say, "Not Dean Fleming, he drives a red Trans Am," but I was afraid that maybe Rae saw him as the boy version of herself. Her face came at me. She kissed me right on the mouth. Her lips were moist and tasted of cookies. She stopped and looked at my face and kissed me again. "How was that?" she asked.

What was I supposed to say? You can kiss good? Dean can kiss good?

She narrowed her eyes for a second, thinking. "Be Harley Tucker," she said. I didn't want to be Harley Tucker. He was skinny and he slicked his hair back with butch wax like he was trying to be Elvis or something. But I couldn't say no. I had to be somebody, some boy. Rae tipped her head back, eyes closed. I moved to kiss her, not thinking of Harley Tucker at all. When our lips touched, she threw her arms around my shoulders and pulled me in tight. I moved my head around, trying to make this kiss spectacular. I figured I'd give her one of those French kisses I'd heard the boys talk about. Harley would, I thought. I slid the tip of my tongue into Rae's mouth. She quit moving for a second, then shimmied out of my arms. "Har-ley," she sang. She kissed me on the cheek, took my hands in hers, and began swinging me around in circles. She held her face toward the sky, laughing. Sun sparkled in her hair. Her hands warmed me. We were dancers, spinning together. Not sinking but rising. Hand in hand, we whirled round and round and round and round, and I quit being a girl whose mother tried to drown her, quit worrying about what Mama would think—quit thinking, period. I was naked. Beneath the sky.

. . . . .

The next day, I couldn't wait to see Rae, to throw my clothes off again, to pretend to be a boy and kiss her, to spin naked beneath the lacy branches of trees. When the last bell rang at school, kids scrambled around us in the hall to get outside. Rae grabbed my arm, pulled me in close and breathed into my ear, "Meet me later. You know where." I wanted to do more than meet her; I wanted to run away from home and live in that shack with her. Never wear clothes again.

An hour later, Maisey and I stood in the kitchen, arguing over her old tore-up bike.

"You're always riding off on my bicycle," Maisey said. "You act like it's yours."

James watched *Batman*, the TV blaring: doodoo doodoo doodoo doodoo, doodoo doodoo doodoo doodoo. *Batman.* The Penguin was about to drop Batman and Robin into a vat of acid.

"C'mon, Maisey," I said. "You never even use it." I knew I was about to wear her down—she started gnawing on her fingernails—when suddenly Mama swooped down from nowhere like a vulture and landed between us. I'd forgotten she was home. She'd been taking a nap, which was always a bad sign. Her face was creased from lying on the covers. Her red hair stuck up in tufts on one side of her head. "Goddammit, you want to fight?" she asked, her eyes squinched up. "I'll make you fight." Her jaw quivered.

She dug her fingers into my arm and dragged me into the middle of the dining room, stood me in front of the TV on the big rope rug. Out of the corner of my eye I saw the words *Wham! Bam!* flash across the TV screen. Batman and Robin were going to get away, and so was Maisey, who was sniveling, trying to sneak out the back door. Mama jerked Maisey's arm and hauled her over next to me. "Now you stand there," she said to Maisey in a low voice, and she ran to the back of the house to get Daddy's belt.

Maisey and I stood still, one skinny body in front of the other, waiting to see what was going to happen; we didn't want to fight anymore. James said, "Why don't y'all move over; I'm watching *Batman*."

Mama charged back down the hall toward us, screaming, "Turn that damn TV off before I kick a hole in it." Nobody moved. Mama jerked the cord out of the wall and whipped it hard against the floor, trying to break the black plastic plug. Her whole face was pinched now, as though she was going to cry. The plug didn't break, and that just made her madder. She tossed the cord down and turned toward us, twisting the leather belt high in one hand, like she was going to swing at us, then lowered her voice to a growl. "You want to fight? Hit each other."

James started to get up, and Mama shoved him back on the couch. "You are going to sit right here and watch. I'm sick of you children fighting. Now fight. Lily; you hit Maisey or I'm going to whip you both till your legs bleed."

I was scared and looked down at the rug, the way the blue and green and brown strands ran in circles; I wondered why the rug didn't come unraveled. I thought of Rae and me dancing naked beneath the big blue sky. Swinging each other in circles.

Maisey edged away from me, but then Mama hit her skinny leg and she whimpered and socked me in the arm, then Mama whipped the belt against my thigh so I kicked Maisey and we both started crying. Not because we were hurting each other—we were fighting like girls—but because Mama was running around us with the belt like a dog chasing its tail.

When Maisey didn't hit me back, Mama jerked a handful of her hair and Maisey closed her eyes and kicked at me but she wasn't close enough. Mama hung on to Maisey's hair like she was hanging on to a baby doll and with her other hand, swung the belt at me and started screaming again, "Hit each other, goddammit, hit each other or I'm going to kill you both."

Out of the corner of my eye I could see James hunched on the black couch.

Maisey and I repelled each other the way magnets do if you don't line then up just right. It wasn't funny anymore. I felt like we were both naked, and not like Rae and I had been. This was an ugly dance, and I was ashamed and I wanted Mama to stop, to leave us alone, but she wouldn't stop until we hurt each other, we had to hurt each other, so I kicked at my sister's legs like a wild woman, just stop, stop, stop, stop, stop, stop.

Mama was about to grab Maisey again and Maisey slapped her right in the face. Mama's eyes turned into giant zeroes for a second, then she dropped to her knees and started crying and holding her cheek. Strands of Maisey's hair stuck to her fingers. The room went completely quiet except for the horrible sound of Mama crying.

I just stood there until it hit me—you don't slap your mama, no matter what—so I balled up my fist and punched Maisey square on the cheek. It felt good to hit her, to smash the bone behind her soft skin. I kicked her as hard as I could, then grabbed her, threw her onto the floor, and plopped down on her stomach. I pinned her stringy arms down with my knees, frogged her belly with knotted fists. I wanted to kill her; she was the cause of our unhappiness; she made Mama do this to us. James crouched behind me, trying to lug me off of Maisey, but I punched and slapped her wiry little body till my palms stung, my fingers covered with snot and tears.

8

After Mama made me and Maisey beat each other up, I never told Rae anything about what happened at my house again. She wanted to know why I didn't show up that day, but how could you tell someone that your Mama made you kick your sister till she had purple bruises running up and down her legs? I didn't even tell Daddy when he came home that day, not even after he asked me for the third time what was wrong. The house was full of bad air. I wished Mama would just go on and go crazy and go live at the hospital with the patients, since she liked them so much.

The hospital had become Mama's home in a way. After Thanksgiving, she spent hours at our house cutting angels and snowmen and trumpets out of cardboard, spraying them with fake snow, sprinkling glitter on them. Then she hauled them up to her ward and tacked them on the walls for the patients. Her patient friends thought she was Michelangelo. Mama introduced them to me once when Daddy and I came to pick her up from work. Mrs. Sylvester was a tiny woman with a birdlike face that peeked out from beneath a cloud of lavender hair. She was from Miami Beach, and she spent all her time crocheting lace doilies she gave to Mama. Mrs. Vanatter was a refrigerator-sized woman from Tampa who wrote poetry. Standing next to each other, they looked like a giant and a dwarf. Mrs. Sylvester grabbed my hand with her claw. "Honey," she wheezed, "I've been in museums all over the world, seen the finest art, the Renoirs, the Rembrandts, the Picassos. Your mother," she said, giving my hand a squeeze, "is an artist of the first order. Her snowmen are positively cold."

Mrs. Vanatter nodded. "She could work for Hallmark."

"Those women have style," Mama said on the ride home. "You won't catch them sitting around in their nightgowns." She turned around in her seat to look me full in the face, her eyes all dreamy. "Mrs. Sylvester used to be a millionaire," she said. "Can you imagine? She and her husband owned a hotel shaped like an ocean liner in Miami Beach, but they lost it because Mr. Sylvester went berserk one day at Hialeah and bet a zillion dollars on a horse named Hooves of Fire."

Mama said that even though Mrs. Sylvester didn't have a pot to pee in, she could get a little snobby sometimes from all those years of being a bigwig; she'd forget she was in the hospital and try to boss the nurses around. Mama still liked Mrs. Sylvester, but she cared the most for Mrs. Vanatter. She had a black satin purse full of Mrs. Vanatter's work, pages and pages of poetry.

"Look at that writing," Mama said when she brought the poems home. "How could you think anyone was crazy who has such beautiful handwriting?"

I looked at the writing; it was beautiful, the letters perfectly shaped and slanted. The poems were all about flowers and sunshine and rain and hummingbirds, and Mama crammed them into that old pocketbook she didn't use anymore, and it was sad in a way, all those poems shoved into a closet. But Mama said Mrs. Vanatter writes her poems every day all day; she sits by a window and writes and writes and writes. Sometimes she doesn't even eat. She has notebooks full of poems about daisies, Mama said.

Rae would've found a way to laugh about those things. She seemed to live just outside of her life, able to watch it the way her Mama watched wrestling on TV. Nothing seemed to bother her. People were made for her amusement. Even her old Mama.

Mrs. Miller attended the holy roller church a mile down the street from my house, where she spoke in tongues. "You don't want to miss that," Rae said. "When Mama gets the spirit and starts babbling, she can make a drowning look tame."

So I told Mama I wanted to go to the Baptist church, and come Sunday morning I got dressed, and walked up the street in the cold toward the First Baptist, then walked on around the block and back down the street to the Assembly of God. It was nothing like the church Mama and Daddy drug me and James and Maisey to on those Sundays when Mama felt like facing a crowd.

For one thing, it was the smallest church I'd ever seen, all wooden inside like a playhouse. A smell like mothballs seeped from the floor. The pews were as hard as the benches from a picnic table. Rae and I sat down with Mrs. Miller between us. The preacher stepped up to the front of the church and made a few announcements. Then he picked up his Bible, riffled the pages, and launched into his sermon as if he'd become somebody else. He started out preaching slowly, then revved himself into a kind of frenzy, the same way Mama did that day when she sicced me and Maisey on each other like dogs. He gripped the Bible in his thick white fingers like a hatchet, chopping at the air. Sweat ran down the sides of his big red face even though the church was icy-cold. I stared straight ahead, too afraid to move.

The preacher's words poured out like scalding water: "You will buuuuurn in hay-yell if you do not take the Lord Jesus Christ to be your Savior. You can be rich, you can be poor, you can be pretty as a peach or ugly as bulldog, but GodtheFather won't have none of ya, less you take the Lord Jesus Christ into your heart." His voice got louder and louder till he was purely barking at us to Get! Up! And! Do! Something! Almost every person in the church was shouting out now, "Save me, Jesus," "Oh Lord God Almighty," "Amen brother."

I watched as a woman in a faded blue dress threw her hands up to the ceiling and bawled, "Oh Jesus." Then something twitched in her and words started gurgling out of her mouth, "Oh gubba gubba, Jesus God, gubba gubba," her whole body shaking like she was strapped to a washing machine going full tilt. Others around me, men in worn-out overalls, women with hair spun high over their heads like cotton candy, started shouting and moaning. The whole church heaved from side to side with swaying bodies. The room stank of sweat. I was terrified.

Then Mrs. Miller got the spirit and rose, trembling, out of the pew next to me. Rae leaned back and nodded, grinning at me. Mrs. Miller flung her flabby arms up to heaven, and her eyes turned white like a snake's eyes do when it's shedding its skin, but she wasn't holding still like a shedding snake. She started hollering and screaming and threw herself out into the aisle on the pine floor, where she writhed around like she was on fire. I thought she was having a fit, that she'd gone out of her mind for real. Rae moved closer to me, whispered in my ear, "Every Sunday."

Meanwhile, the preacher started slowing things down with his voice, saying about one word to the five he was shouting out before, while the people quieted themselves down, whimpering and catching their breath the way little kids do when they've been crying hard. He mopped his big wet face with a handkerchief. All over the church, people fanned themselves, patted at their bodies. An old woman walked over and helped Mrs. Miller to her feet. "We are God's people," the preacher said slowly, his voice spent. "We are the chosen ones. Now let us pray."

I wasn't about to close my eyes. Mrs. Miller stood next to me, her head bent, her eyes wide open. She picked at something on her dress. I wondered right then if I'd trade Mama's meanness for Mrs. Miller's fits, and I wasn't sure I could say yes.

By the time we walked outside into the glare of the sun, the people had turned normal again. Talking about the ham left cooking in the oven back home. The sale at the Dollar Store. The preacher combed his hair, shook people's hands.

Rae and I stood off to the side. "It really ain't so weird," she said, pulling her coat close around her body. "Remember that story Mrs. Gambil read to us, 'Young Goodman Brown?' That's what it reminds me of, except they're worshipping God, not the devil."

"Yeah," I said. I looked at the people standing on the grass in the sun. I thought of the story Mrs. Gambil had read to our class. How people had these secret lives. Mama had one. I had one. Daddy did too. I figured most of the patients in the hospital had secret lives. But they'd let the secret out and look what happened to them. Locked up. Who knew who was who? How did people ever find the true heart of themselves?

. . . . .

I guess I was bound sooner or later to find Rae's hidden self, at least the one she hid from me. On the following Monday, I rode up to her house and her daddy came out on the porch before I even knocked, and I wondered if what Maisey had said was true: that he had x-ray eyes.

I looked closely at him. His eyes were dark brown with flecks of green and he had a woman's long eyelashes. He squinted at me. "Something wrong?"

"No," I said. Before I could ask him where Rae was, he told me she wasn't home. He waved his brown hand toward the yard, said Rae was down the road somewhere. So I pedaled out to the shack where we played, got off the bike and leaned it up against a sweet gum tree. Rae's bike and one other rusted out bike lay in the grass. I heard voices from inside.

I walked to the side of the house, stepped up on a concrete block, and peeped in one of the smudged windows. Two boys sat on the floor, watching as Rae slipped her shirt on over her head. She held her hand out to them. Whatever had happened was over. I moved away from the window to the corner of the house. The door opened and the two boys stumbled onto the porch, laughing, pushing against each other. I recognized them from school. Ninth-graders. Too old to be messing with Rae.

Robbie had greasy black hair that was always falling in his dirt-colored eyes. The other boy, Leon, was pale and freckled from head to toe. I didn't *know* them, but I knew who they were. Robbie lived down in River Junction with his mean old grizzled daddy. They lived in a room on top of his daddy's crapped-out old Esso Station. Leon was a boy who wore rat-colored sweaters to school and smelled of sour milk.

I flattened myself against the shack and peeped around the corner at them. When they stepped off the porch, they quit jostling each other and Robbie climbed onto the rusted-out bike, holding it still while Leon hoisted himself onto the handlebars, legs dangling. Then they took off, wobbling down the road like clowns.

I felt awkward, as if I'd shown up uninvited to a party, but I climbed onto the porch anyway. Rae came to the door holding two dollars. "I'm saving up for our trip out west," she said. "Whaddaya think of California? The Pacific Ocean?"

I never asked her what she did to earn the dollars. I didn't want to know.

9

———

The sky was as blue as the paint on a car that December day. Not a single cloud in sight. Perfect. That should've been a sign. You think everything's okay, but really it's not. Rae and I decided to meet at the park that day for a change. Even Maisey came along, although I had to promise her a box of Milk Duds not to tell Mama we'd been with Rae. Maisey knew I sneaked off to see her. I couldn't help but tell her when we lay in bed at night talking before we went to sleep. Rae was the story in my life.

We raked up pine straw with our fingers, built a make-believe house, outlined rooms in the grass. Rae and I took turns being the husband and wife. Maisey was our little girl. Rae stood in the doorway of our straw house and shouted, "Honey, I'm home," and Maisey and I rushed toward her. In a voice pitched as high and sweet as I could manage, I asked, "Did you have a good day at work?"

I couldn't wait for my turn to be the husband. I hated how my voice sounded when I tried to be the wife. The husband didn't have to gush over anything; he just got to walk into the house like a normal person, sit down, and wait for his wife to bring him something, anything.

That afternoon Rae and I decided to make Maisey take a nap so we could practice kissing on each other. Rae and I were going to take turns being the man. The man would be in charge of the kiss. Before we could decide who was going to be the man first, though, Maisey said the thought of Rae and me kissing made her want to puke. "I'm gonna tell Mama," she said. She kicked a hole in the wall of her straw bedroom and ran home. I didn't care. *Let her tell*, I thought.

Rae got to be the man first. She led me into the bedroom of our straw house and pushed me down on our imaginary bed. She laughed as she dropped down in the grass next to me, then leaned over my face. She pinned my arms down. She was so still I could see her heartbeat pulsing in that soft spot just beneath her ear. "Close your eyes," she said. I did. I felt her leaning closer to me, felt her warm breath on my cheek, smelled the sweaty salt on her neck, the pine sap on her hands. She touched her tongue to my lips and it was such a strange, hot and wet feeling that I felt myself falling right through the ground. It was as if she felt me falling, too, and scared herself, for in the next second she brushed her lips against my mouth and gave me one of those old-lady smooches I hated so much.

When it was my turn to be the man, I pushed her down and held her against the grass. I kept my eyes open and kissed her softly on the lips, lingering only long enough to notice how perfect her white eyelashes and eyebrows were. Tiny blue veins crisscrossed beneath her skin. I pushed the tip of my tongue between her lips like I did the day we danced naked. For a second I floated above that heat. Then

Rae popped up. "Lilllly! No! You always do that. We're just practicing." She stood up. "Let's go do something else."

I spun her into a blur on the merry-go-round, running in tight circles until I got dizzy. Then I stepped back and watched as she whizzed by, smiling, her eyes shut, her hair blown back. I wished I could kiss her again.

Later on a couple of boys came to play. Robbie and Leon, the same boys I'd seen coming out of our shack that day. They trotted onto the playground like stray dogs sniffing dirt on their way somewhere else. They ran at the merry-go-round, shouting and laughing. Robbie jumped up next to Rae; Leon grabbed the metal bar and ran in circles. Every time he passed me, I saw an old green bruise the size of a half-dollar on his pale freckled cheek.

Rae didn't mind the boys; she knew them better than I did, even though they were older. After spinning on the merry-go-round, she was just as charged up as they were. She leapt off the whirling metal platform and bolted through the grass toward the swings, glancing over her shoulder at the boys tearing after her. I walked behind them, feeling clumsy, wondering when they were going to leave so I could have Rae to myself again.

Instead of sitting on the swings, the boys flung them, chains rattling, up over the rusted metal bar again and again until the chains shortened and the swings dangled high off the ground. Rae sat in the dirt and watched, then the boys flopped down next to her, rolling their bodies one way, then another, bumping against her every now and then, muttering, "C'mon baby, oh, baby, oh, honey," howling with laughter. I sat on the grass and watched them roll and jump and howl. They ignored me.

Leon flattened himself out in the dirt, his eyes closed, his lips pooched out like Elvis's. He began moaning and humming, moving his skinny hips up and down. "Ohh, Rae, uhn, Rae, uhnn. Baby. Let's do it in the bushes. C'mon baby, show me your titties like ya did the other day." Rae looked over at me and rolled her eyes. I wasn't surprised by his words—boys were always trying to shock us—like last year when Rick Horton carved the word *fuck* into his desk at school, and all the fifth grade boys paraded by to look at it, like there was something real there, something besides the letters f-u-c-k.

Robbie laughed, reached over, and tugged on Rae's foot. "Stop, you idiot," she said, looking away from him. "You're such a moron." Then they quieted down—Leon quit his humming, quit jerking his hips, and rolled over to face Rae. Bits of dried yellow grass stuck up off his head.

Robbie sat up. Pushed his greasy black hair out of his eyes. Both boys leaned in close, ready to bargain. I could barely hear their low thrumming voices, but imagined what they were saying. *Show us yours and we'll show you ours,* the words soft and round. Rae looked at me as if to say, *You wanna come?* but I shook my head no, fast. And so the boys talked Rae into walking to the corner of the field that dropped down a hill and out of sight.

I was mad at Rae for walking away from me without a word, for the way she sauntered off with those boys. I wanted to throw a rock at her dusty back as she ambled across the field; I wanted to break those boys' grimy hands so they couldn't touch Rae; I wanted to break her hands so she couldn't touch them. I sat there for a moment feeling sorry for myself, then it hit me that Rae had gone off with two older boys and I panicked. I could hear Mama's voice: *Stay away from the big boys, Lily, they might hurt you.*

I got up and walked quickly to the edge of the field. The low hum of voices stopped me at a distance. That and the sight of Rae, lying half-naked in the grass, a twisted look on her face. I squatted in the dirt. Rae's legs looked so white beneath that blue sky. Leon kneeled next to her, his bruised face close to hers, his hands pressing her arms to the ground, just as mine had earlier. Was he going to kiss her? Was he holding her down? Robbie, standing off to the side, unzipped his pants and let them fall into a rumpled pile he kicked aside. I could see his milky-white ass. He stepped closer to Rae and she jerked against Leon. She screamed, "Lilllly!" Leon moved his hand over her mouth.

I started to call out her name, too, but was afraid the boys would grab me next. I didn't want to play this game. She'd started it. I jumped up and ran toward my house, blood beating in my ears, *Raeraeraeraeraeraerae.* I passed the church of the dead goats. I passed the church where Rae's Mama had thrown herself on the floor. When I got to Satsuma Street, I slowed to a walk. I didn't want anyone to see me running, didn't want anyone to think I'd done anything wrong. Dry yellow leaves fluttered across the sidewalk. A gray bird startled me, flying out of a green tangle of morning-glory vines. Bright purple blossoms fell to the ground. I almost cried. A voice in my head wouldn't let me. *She walked across the field with them. She did. I wanted to throw rocks at her. She walked across the field with them, she didshedidshedidshedid.*

When I got home, my ears were filled with a tinny sound. Mama stood over the garbage can in the kitchen peeling potatoes for supper. The faucet was dripping, *plip, plip, plip*, so loud I wanted to scream, *Stop that noise!* Maisey snapped green beans at the sink. She waved one at my face and smirked, as if she had a secret. Behind her head, the window over the sink was foggy with grime. Mama filled a pot with water and turned to look at me. I stood next to Maisey, trying to slow my breath down. Sweat slid down my back. "I didn't do anything," I said.

"What's wrong? Somebody after you?" Mama clanged the lid on the pot and turned to look at me again. My head filled with images of the boys and Rae. Her white legs beneath that blue sky. The pale boy's hand on her mouth. Tears rose up into my eyes, and I swallowed hard to make them go away.

Mama kneeled in front of me. "I got your number now, Lily. You go near that Miller girl again and I'm going to beat you to within an inch of your life. That's girl's nothing but trouble, and her mama and daddy are just plain trash." She turned away from me. Maisey started humming.

I knew then that Maisey told her what we'd been doing. I wanted to tell Mama what I saw, what had happened, but I knew I couldn't say anything. If I said anything, I'd just be getting myself into trouble one way or another. But I wanted to describe the boys and Rae and the grass and the sky, and I wanted Mama to tell me what I saw. I wanted her to tell me that nothing happened. Daddy would. He would hear my story, and then he'd say, *You didn't do anything because nothing happened. She walked across the field with them, honey. Nothing happened. The sky was as blue as the paint on a car. Not a cloud in sight.*

10

Rae wasn't at school for the next few days. When she came back a couple of days before Christmas vacation, she walked past me in the dark, crowded hall as if she couldn't see me, but I knew she could see me out of the corner of her eye. I stood still in the middle of a swarm of kids. I could smell the cold air on their sweaters. Even though Mama told me she'd kill me if I played with Rae anymore, it didn't matter, she wanted to kill me anyway. When I got close enough to Rae to ask her to meet me after school, she lowered her eyes, whispering no, and let herself be swept away into the crowd of kids moving down the hall. Her white hair hung in limp strands over her shoulders.

I missed her, but I didn't want to miss her. I kept seeing Leon with the ugly green bruise on his face, except now the bruise was yellow and I hated him. I hated him, because he'd stolen Rae from me. Turned her into a shadow.

I sat at my hard wooden desk surrounded by kids I'd never fit in with and stared at the crinkled up map of the world hanging on the wall next to the blackboard. The world was divided into crescents like segments of an orange.

Countries were yellow or pink or green. Oceans, seas, lakes, and rivers blue. Mountain ranges brown. Florida was a pale green finger separating the Atlantic Ocean from the Gulf of Mexico. Chattahoochee was a dot of red. All those dots were where people lived, and where they lived decided what kind of life they had. We had a whole world to choose from, and I wondered why we ended up where we do. Why did I end up in a town where the main business was keeping people locked up? Trapped? Why couldn't I have been born in Tierra del Fuego, where people used to carry fire from place to place because they were afraid of being cold?

I finally just walked up to Rae in the lunchroom; I could feel a blur of faces watching me as I crossed the room, and I wondered if everyone knew what had happened. The lunchroom was filled with a greasy-smelling cloud that turned my stomach. I wanted to drop my plastic tray and run out the door. Instead, I slid the tray onto the table. The loud clatter of metal forks and spoons rattled in my ears.

Rae kept her eyes lowered. I'd never seen her like this. I sat down. "Are you okay?" I asked. She looked away from me and made a face as if to say, *"Why in God's name are you asking me that?"*

"I'm sorry," I said. "I was scared."

She looked at me then, hard. "What are you talking about? Sorry? Why in the hell are you sorry?"

"Because..."

"Because I had some fun with some boys and you didn't?" She pushed her tray across the table, glanced at me, then looked away. "Lily, you know something? You're one stupid girl."

I was confused. I thought back to the day at the park,

Leon kneeling next to Rae, his head close to her face, his hands pressing her arms to the ground, just as mine had earlier. Robbie, standing off to the side, his pants unzipped, his milky-white ass. Rae screamed my name and Leon moved his hand over her mouth. I knew what I'd seen.

Rae looked around the lunchroom, her eyes settling on a couple of girls a couple of tables over. They stared at us. She smirked at them and said, "Take a picture; it lasts longer." Then she turned to me. "You always get things wrong, Lily. Think about it. Things aren't always the way they seem. I never wanted to kiss you." She rubbed the table with her thumb. "I don't have time to be your stupid girlfriend." She narrowed her eyes at me, lowered her voice to a whisper. "And your stupid drowning that you go on and on about. Think about it. You fell in the water and your crazy-assed Mama, who can't even swim, jumped in and saved you. But is that the way you see it? Hell no. You think she tried to drown you. Nothing happened to you, Lily. Nothing happened to me. Nobody does anything to me that I don't want them to. Nobody messes with me, so don't come saying you're sorry to me. You don't know shit."

11

A few days later I woke up and decided to be a boy. I didn't know shit. I did not know shit. I was tired of being Lily. A stupid damn girl. I figured if a person could make things disappear by acting like they never happened, then I could make something come true by acting like it did happen.

No more wishing. Boys could do whatever they wanted and get away with it. They could punch you in the nose. They could be heroes. If I'd been a boy that day Rae walked off, I could've saved her and she would've walked off with me. She wouldn't have to act like nothing happened, because nothing would've happened.

I cut my hair short and Mama smiled as if she'd finally gotten the girl she wanted. She brushed her hand across my forehead as she whispered, "Your pixie looks cute." She must've thought I wanted to be Twiggy or something. But my hair did look fine once I slicked it back with some water. For the next couple of weeks I did boy things. I snuck into the bathroom and practiced shaving, lathering my face with Ivory soap, scraping the foam off with a yellow pencil. I stole a pair of James's underwear and practiced peeing like a boy, straddling the toilet seat and peeing toward the back. I dreamed about Rae, rescued her from those boys and was given kisses on my cheek. I told Maisey and James to call me Tommy. They looked at me like I was stupid and I knew I was but I couldn't help it.

That winter I asked for a Schwinn Stingray at the same time James did, and come Christmas morning, I thought for sure I'd get one to make up for the Christmas when I got this lousy red cowgirl skirt with a dumb looking fringed blouse and a pair of white patent-leather cowgirl boots. I couldn't even bring myself to try that junk on.

The bike was parked next to the tree in the living room, red and shiny as a fire truck. But no, just as soon as I threw my leg over the banana seat, leaned back against the sissy bar, and grabbed hold of the apehanger handlebars, here comes Mama with James, his dark brown hair all flattened out on one side of his head, sleep in his eyes. Mama piped up and said, "No, Lily, that's James's. That's a boy's bike," she said, lowering her voice to a growl. "Your Barbie doll is over there."

"A Barbie doll?" I said, shocked. "I'm twelve years old. I don't want a stupid Barbie doll. I don't play with dolls; I've never played with dolls."

"I know that," Mama said. "It's not for you to play with. That's an original Fashion Queen Barbie. She'll be worth something one day," she said, "if you take good care of her. That Barbie's as good as money in the bank." She pushed me toward it, then turned and walked into the kitchen to help Daddy fix breakfast.

James smirked at me as he climbed onto the bike. "Stop stealing my underwear," he said. "Dork." He grabbed hold of the handlebars, and I stood there in shock, couldn't believe this was happening again.

I had *asked* for that bike, and Mama had shoved me toward an old Barbie doll that wore pearl earrings. It was like she was saying, *You are going to be the Right Kind of Girl, and this is what the Right Kind of Girls want.* It was bad enough just being a girl, much less having a mother who thought I'd want a stupid Barbie. Not even to play with, but to keep safe so she'd be worth something.

James hopped off the bike and sneered at me again. "Don't even touch it," he said. "It's mine." I lunged at him and punched him square in the belly. His eyes went round and he doubled over. I slammed my fists so hard against his curved back that I hurt myself, but that didn't stop him. He reared up and flew at me, knocked me down into the pile of presents and wrapping paper strewn across the floor. I landed funny on a metal tackle box and felt blood trickling down my leg. I squirmed away from James, grabbed the Barbie doll by the legs, jumped up and whacked him as hard as I could across his nose. That surprised him.

He pounced on me again, then began punching my chest with balled-up fists, tears running down his cheeks. His breath smelled like peppermint. "You're not a boy," he screamed as he pummeled me, "you're just a stupid fucking girl, a stupid fucking girl, a stupid fucking girl."

I spit in his face. "You're a stupid fucking sissy," I shouted. Maisey tried to get between us, but James and I were going to kill each other. I was ready to murder him. Finally, Mama ran back into the room screaming at us to stop. Daddy stood in the doorway behind her, holding a frying pan. The smell of bacon filled the room.

73

"She hit me in the face with that Barbie doll," James cried, his fingers covering his nose.

Mama swung around, picked the Barbie up, grabbed me by the arm and wailed away at the backs of my legs. "You have to ruin everything, don't you, Lily?" My legs stung, but I wasn't going to let Mama know it. I glared at her when she stopped. "You're not going to stop until you make me have a nervous breakdown, are you?" she said.

She threw the Barbie doll across the room. "Now both of you, get up and get the hell out of this house before I kill you." She watched us while we got up and gathered our stuff together, then turned and pushed through the door. Daddy stood still, holding the frying pan. "Put that wrapping paper in the trash," he said, as if that had anything to do with our fight.

I hated James when he rolled his bike outside and sailed down the hill barefooted, still wearing his red flannel pajamas beneath his jacket. Even his pajamas made me mad; they were covered with spaceships, airplanes, cowboys, Indians. I had to wear a stupid pink gown, and nobody could ride a bike down the street wearing a gown. I didn't feel better until later that morning when I slung Barbie on top of the house and watched her roll off the roof into the azaleas. When I reached into the bushes to grab her so I could throw her on the roof again, I spotted an old plastic washtub and realized I could sit in that and slide down the driveway. Our driveway was steep, so steep that the tail end of our Fairlane would drag against it if Daddy didn't pull in just right.

Sliding down the hill in the washtub was almost as good as riding a bicycle, but not quite. It was loud for one thing, sounded like somebody sanding a piece of wood. And I could feel every crack in the concrete on my butt, which was still sore from landing on that tackle box during the fight. I skinned my knuckles raw before I wore a hole in the tub. Then I was stuck. But after watching James ride his new bike around the house and down the hill for the three-hundredth time, I got another idea. I would coast down the hill on my old blue tricycle.

That trike was like part of my body, and I knew just how to handle it. I hauled it out of the utility room and parked it on the carport, right at the crest of the hill. Maisey dropped her Barbies to watch me, to see what I was going to do. I was way too big to ride it, so I stood on the little metal step between the back wheels and leaned over to grasp the handlebars. I pushed the trike forward a little, braked it by dragging my foot, then did it again. Except for the fact that I couldn't sit on it, it was perfect. I'd surf that baby down the hill. I took off. The next thing I knew, I was gone. I never had a chance to put my foot down. The wheels spun so fast it was like they weren't even there.

The peppery smell of crushed weeds rose around me as I lay in the ditch at the bottom of the hill crumpled up under the blue tricycle, our fuzzy-headed neighbor, Mrs. Dozier, looking over her shoulder at me as she pinned her husband's boxer shorts on a clothesline. Her eyes were so close together she looked like a hamster.

Every now and then she glanced over her shoulder at me as she clipped a shirt onto the clothesline. I lay in the ditch and watched her watching me. I thought of Rae lying in that field, her naked white legs, me watching the boy move his hand over her mouth. Me running home in a blur. I thought of other blurry things, of how the tricycle spokes disappeared

75

in a blur, how when you're going really fast in a car, all the bushes blur together, how my mother hated me, how when you're a girl who likes to do boy things, everything's a blur. I lay in the ditch whimpering for myself, a blur rolling down the hill.

Finally, Mama walked down the hill to get me. I heard her voice before I saw her. "Mrs. Dozier, you didn't see Evel Knievel whiz by, did you?" Mrs. Dozier said something, but I couldn't make it out. I heard Mama's voice again, cheerful: "Oh, that's a lovely tablecloth; do you think the sun will bleach all those ugly stains out?" Mama didn't like Mrs. Dozier one little bit.

Then Mama stood at the edge of the ditch, looking down at me. "Are you crazy?" she whispered as loud as she could. "What do you think you are? A damn stunt driver? I oughta leave your ass here, let the ants eat you." But she bent over, gripped my hand, and dragged me out of the ditch, up over the weeds, and up the hill to the house, saying over and over again, "Oh, honey, if a car had been coming, you would've been killed." And she said it so many times— ifacarhadbeencoming, ifacarhadbeencoming—that it started sounding like a wish and I thought she was saying "if only a car had been coming, if only..." and I saw the car coming, as if she'd wished it into being. I saw it rolling right over me in slow motion, not a blur at all, and I knew that I'd almost been killed, that I would've been killed, if a car had been coming. If a car had been coming, I would've been killed. And Mama would've been happy. And it was all because I was a girl who wanted a banana-seat bicycle.

12

A *few days* later, I told Mama I was going to ride uptown to the Dimestore, but I was really going to ride out to mine and Rae's shack to see what it felt like. Mama was still mad at me for whacking James and pretending to be a boy, but I didn't care. Every time I looked at the purple bruise on James's nose, I felt giddy, wanted to hit him again. Let him have that stupid Stingray. Who needed a sissy bar anyway? Not me.

I rode Maisey's rickety bike through town, pedaled my boy-self past all the dusty shop windows, slowing so I could get a good look at my reflection in the glass. I didn't have the delicate features of a girl. Not my nose, not my lips, not even my dark eyebrows. I would've thought I was a boy if I saw myself pedaling by. I thought back to a day at school when Amy Melzer, a tall blond fourteen-year-old, cornered me in the hall at school, looked at me with slitted eyes, and said, "You woulda made a good-looking boy." She smiled and I turned red. Later, I wished I'd said something back to her, like *You wanna kiss or something?*

I was a good-looking boy. Dark brown hair, olive skin.

A mouth I could twist into a sneer like Elvis's. I spit on the sidewalk and pedaled on. I pulled up to the Dimestore and leaned my bike against the crumbling brick wall. The bell jangled when the door slapped shut behind me. It was dark inside. Old Mrs. Bevis sat behind the counter watching me. I said hi and pretended to look for a bag of Sugar Babies— "I don't see the Sugar Babies; where are the Sugar Babies? Don't you have any Sugar Babies?"—while I stole a pack of gum with her looking straight at me. I could've robbed a bank right then.

I climbed onto my bike and headed out into the country, down the dirt road to Rae's. I knew she wouldn't be home. I'd heard that the Millers had gone up to Macon to visit Rae's cousin. From the road the gray house looked hollow, empty as a shell. The grass that Rae had laid down in to let her pony walk over her had dried up and blown away. It was hard to believe that come spring, the yard would be full of dandelions.

Rae and I used to make wishes with the dandelions; we blew the white puff of seeds hard until each one floated off in the wind. You weren't supposed to say your wish out loud, but we did. We wanted the same thing: to live together in California when we grew up and own a toy store.

I rode past her house on down the dirt road to our shack. I couldn't bring myself to open the door, so I stood on the porch and looked in through the window. Nothing had changed. A dead spider on the dirty windowsill, a perfect lacy dragonfly wing, one of those dried-up lizards on the wood floor. Off in the corner I saw Rae's blue and gold horse ribbons, the Hav-A-Tampa cigar boxes that held my bug collection. Rae's tap shoes sat on top of the table.

I hopped down and backed away from the house as if it were alive, as if it had swallowed Rae up. I felt myself getting angry at her again for letting those boys into our house, for taking their dollars, for walking away from me that time, for letting that boy do those things to her. But I knew she didn't let him, no matter what she said, and I knew I could've helped her. I could've helped her but I didn't. I didn't because I couldn't tell what was happening, because she walked across the field with them. She did. She walked across the field with them and I couldn't tell. I started to cry. I picked up a rock and, without thinking, threw it through the window, smashing the pane. The pop and clatter of broken glass soothed me, but it wasn't enough. I gathered more rocks and ran around the house, throwing them all, picturing Rae's face at each and every window. By the time I finished, the house was a wreck, the windowpanes nothing but jagged holes, and I realized I'd be in trouble if anyone saw me. I didn't care. Rae was as far gone as one of those dandelion seeds, and I didn't have a prayer of being friends with her again. I punched her out of my head like a window. Just like that. Good-bye.

13

Going back to school after Christmas vacation was the worst time ever. All the kids wore brand-new clothes, and all they wanted to talk about was who got what, and what was I going to say? "Mama got me a collectible Barbie doll." Not that anybody was going to ask, but that didn't make going back any better. I wanted to see Rae. I knew she'd have a field day with all those kids bragging about the loot they got. She could probably come up with a good plan for Fashion Queen Barbie. Tie her to a couple of bottle rockets and shoot her into outer space. Something like that.

James rode his bike ahead of me and Maisey, and I concentrated on hating his guts until he was out of sight. When I got to school, a sick feeling came over me. I remembered Rae's last words to me: "You are one stupid girl, Lily...you don't know shit." I wanted the bell to ring so school would start and I could get it over with.

I didn't see Rae until after lunch. She was sitting on the hill next to the lunchroom with Robbie and Leon, watching the rest of the kids whirl past the way we used to do. She was laughing at something, probably making fun of the girls' new pleated skirts, the boys' blue jeans. I didn't want her to see me. I wondered if she'd been to our shack, seen the broken windows. Wondered if she knew I'd thrown the rocks. I couldn't understand why she'd chosen those boys over me. I watched as Robbie and Leon rolled down the hill away from Rae, bumping into each other, bits of dried grass tossed into the air by their bodies. There wasn't a trace of what had happened that day at the park. They were boys rolling down a hill. She was a girl watching them.

Rae and I just stopped being friends. She never said another word about the boys after that day in the lunchroom. She never let herself get near me again. It was as though we'd never met, as though we'd never gotten naked together and danced beneath the sky. I disappeared, became one of the rest of the kids, and she became one of *them*, girls who didn't follow the rules. She started hanging out with the rough kids, not just Robbie and Leon but Sharon Etheridge, a girl whose arms were covered with small pink craters from cigarette burns, and Mike Jones, a big fat stupid kid who once hyperventilated on a dare and fell backward on the iron radiator in homeroom, knocking himself out.

I found myself being pulled into the crowd of regular kids. A few of the girls circled me in the bathroom. I knew they didn't want to be friends, they just wanted to know *Was it true? Did she really?* I didn't know what story to tell so I just shrugged my shoulders and said "I don't know."

But a story got told anyway, how before Christmas, Rae's daddy drove down to the Esso Station and accused those River Junction boys of doing something. Some thing. Some terrible thing. They said he knocked the door right off its hinges. Grabbed Robbie by the throat. Threatened to kill somebody. But she wanted to do it, the girls all said. Why else would she have gone off with them? Everybody knew that. Rae told me herself. *You don't know shit, Lily.*

She started smoking cigarettes on top of the hill behind the shop class with those boys. I tried to get her attention; I started hanging out at the bottom of the hill where Mr. Ryals, the shop teacher, tossed splintered boards, dumped piles of pale yellow sawdust. I bummed cigarettes from Sharon Etheridge, puffed hard on them, blew smoke rings in Rae's direction, but she wouldn't look at me. And when she did, her eyes slid right over me, like water, as if I weren't even there.

14

Mrs. Miller disappeared in late March and the police found her roaming through the pine woods near the Georgia side of Lake Seminole in nothing but a silky white slip covered with beggar's-lice. She told them she was on her way to swim the Living Waters of the Holy Ghost. To get to the other shore where Jesus was waiting for her with a white gown and a pair of gauzy wings. She was going to fly right out of there. I could see her, standing on the shore of Lake Seminole, dressed in white, those big gauzy wings stuck on her back. She'd take one last whiff of that fishy-smelling air and start flapping those wings back and forth till her feet slowly lifted off the sandy shore. She'd be wobbly at first— she'd roll to one side, then the other—but by the time she got high enough to see the whole town of Chattahoochee beneath her, she'd have the hang of it and she'd glide on a thermal, smooth as one of those dirty black buzzards I was always seeing way up in the sky. Circling over Chattahoochee like it was a dead thing.

She wasn't the first person to try to escape Chattahoochee. Once a patient snuck out of the hospital and swam clear across the lake in his pajamas, but the guards were waiting for him on the other shore. And once a boy named Russell drank too many beers and swam halfway across before his legs cramped up. His cousins stood in a warm puddle of water on the dock and watched as he beat the air with his hands and sunk and drowned. They thought he was waving.

There was something about boys; they were supposed to have a force field around them, protecting them from danger. Everybody expected it to work. And it did, most of the time, I think.

At lunch one day, I sat in a warm stripe of sun in the cafeteria and listened as the girls talked. A fly buzzed against the window behind me. The girls drank milk from tiny waxed cartons and choreographed perfect weddings for faraway June days: pastel bridesmaids and flower girls, sunny getaways in sleek black cars. Janine Atwater hummed *I'm going to the chapel and I'm going to get married...."* Then the humming stopped. "Not if you're like that girl Rae." I wanted to shout at them, "I was there. She didn't do anything wrong," but I got the message: nice girls and marriage went together and anything else was pine-straw silly. After a while, you could say, "You're gonna end up like that girl Rae," and everybody knew what you meant.

Mama sure knew what it meant—she always let James go places and do things that she wouldn't dream of letting Maisey and me do, even though he was younger than me. It was like she had it in for us because we were girls. Especially me. Meanwhile, Maisey and I sat home, thumbing through the Sears catalog, *One Life to Live* playing in the background, while James biked out to the lake with Mama's blessings, where he dove off the dock, his slender body free to slice deep water, *because he's a boy, because he's a boy, because he's a boy.*

They took Mrs. Miller to the women's ward where Mama worked. At dinner she whispered about it to Daddy, leaning over her plate, her hand cupped over the corner of her mouth. Then she sat back in her chair, her voice rising. "It took five of us to hold her down, and then the doctor jammed that pink piece of rubber into her mouth. When they hit the electricity, I swear I felt it surge through my arms. I thought it would kill her."

James's ears pricked up. "What, Mama?"

"Nothing. A nervous breakdown," she said.

Maisey asked what a nervous breakdown was.

Mama turned around, surprised. "Why, honey, it really isn't anything. It's when your nerves get shot to hell, when you just can't take it anymore. Something happens. Somebody does something and *bang!*" She slammed her fist down so hard on the table that the plates rattled. "You have a breakdown."

I stopped eating, tried to picture Mrs. Miller strapped to a gurney. I'd heard about those shock treatments. Rae had told me how they tied the patients down and clamped wires on their heads like Frankenstein and pulled a switch. I wondered if the electricity entered Mrs. Miller in a flash of light. I wondered if she thought that jolt was the spirit of God and threw herself on the dirty hospital floor the way she had at church that time, jerking her body around in circles, wildly flinging her arms and legs; I wondered if words just foamed out of her mouth like slobber. Did she speak in tongues?

I wondered how Rae felt, how it felt to have a mother who

really let go and went crazy like a dog with rabies, all because of something you did. *Or because of something someone did to you.* You just took so much, then you fell apart. Like a car rattling down a washboard road in a cloud of red dust near the Apalachicola River, nuts and bolts shaking loose, rusty fenders and muffler dropping into the dirt.

15

Step on a crack, break your mother's back;
Step in a hole, break your mother's sugar bowl.

After Mrs. Miller had her breakdown, I could see that people were lined up like black-and-white dominoes stood on end. Sometimes all it took to topple the whole thing was the slightest touch. When I was six, I found a baby cardinal sitting in the grass under the Japanese plum tree in our backyard, and Mama told me not to touch it; *Its mama won't want it anymore if you touch it,* she said.

But the cat, I wanted to say. I couldn't imagine what would happen to the baby bird if we just left it there. How would it get back into the nest? Pink petals were scattered in the blades of grass beneath the tree. I knelt down to look closer. The bird's heartbeat was visible beneath its thin wrinkly skin. Its feathers were still damp and curled, its eyes tiny gray slits. I laced my hands together to keep myself from picking it up. Then it opened its paper-colored beak and made a thin cheep. I couldn't help it. When Mama wasn't looking, I reached out one finger and touched its feathers.

The next day the bird was dead, tipped over in the grass, its body crawling with shiny black ants, its legs stiff as sticks. I knew I had to dig a hole quick and bury the bird before Mama saw it. She'd know I touched it, that I made its mother leave it to die. I wondered if Rae's mama didn't want her anymore once those boys touched her. I wondered if she'd headed to the water to ask God to forgive her for not wanting her own daughter. I wondered if that might've happened to me.

"As soon as you were born," Mama'd told me once, "the nurses saw you were blue and wrapped you in a rough gray blanket and rubbed your skin hard, and it bothered me, someone else's hands touching your body before mine." I could see her propped up on pillows in a hospital bed, her hands laced together across her belly, watching the nurses work me over.

Why'd you let them touch me if you knew it'd make you not want me anymore? I wanted to ask her. Then, as if she'd heard my question, she said, "I begged them to let me have you, but they ignored me and ran their fat pink palms all over your arms and legs, kneading the blue away. It wasn't until you were pink as a shrimp that they handed you over and I could see that you were all right."

But I wasn't. We weren't. I wasn't even a minute old and I'd already done something to make Mama crazy. I felt like a mistake had been made. Maybe it happened when those nurses rubbed me pink. For a long time after Mama told me that story, I thought being born blue meant I'd been a boy, and that the nurses had turned me into a girl by rubbing me pink. I should've been a little boy blue. Mama would've liked me as much as she liked James. She wouldn't be so mad at me all the time for not wanting to do girl things if I were a boy.

At Easter I went to the hospital auditorium with a group of sixth-graders to sing to the patients. We sang "Up from the Grave He Arose" in rumbling, low-pitched voices. The patients wanted to sing along, and some did, jumping on the words as if they were jumping on a merry-go-round that was already moving. Others sort of hummed or yowled along like dogs whimpering at a painful sound. I sang along, too, but couldn't hear the words; I was all eyes. These people were crazy. They were wearing their pajamas, their hair uncombed. They were slouched in wheelchairs or sitting stiffly on metal fold-up chairs. Some were smiling, some were blank-faced, droop-mouthed, drooling; some rocked back and forth.

Suddenly, a solitary white-haired woman rose to her feet in the back of the room and began dancing, twirling slowly, her pale blue nightgown trailing behind her. She was smiling; she was beautiful. Later, when the hospital staff served us refreshments, I went near her. The skin on her hands and arms was crinkly as wax paper, etched with tiny white stars. She smelled faintly of marigolds and urine. She caught my eye, leaned close to me, and whispered, "My fiancé will be here any minute." I just stared at her. Someone told me later that the woman had been in the hospital most of her life. In 1934, the same year that Bonnie and Clyde died, she'd poured gas on her husband, set him on fire.

That night as I watched Mama fix her hair, I could see how she'd fit in with that audience, see how she'd look in one of those chairs, in one of those nightgowns, telling anyone who came near, "Would you like some orange juice? I was

Miss Florida." You could say anything if you were crazy. Be whoever you wanted to be. Mama knew a patient who thought she was Grace Kelly. And the funny thing, Mama said, was that she was more like Grace Kelly than Grace Kelly was.

Later, when I went to bed, I dreamed I was lying in a grassy field kissing Rae beneath a blue, blue sky. A shadow passed over us like a cloud. It was Mama, towering above us like a giant, blocking out the sun. Then, in the crazy way of dreams, it was night and I was asleep in my room at home and Mama glided in and stood at the foot of my bed in her frowsy cotton nightgown, her body dusted completely white with baby powder, her mouth crammed so full of bobby pins that they fell to the floor like broken teeth when she tried to speak. She just stood there stony-eyed, grinding metal in her mouth.

The next morning, after Daddy left for work, Mama got me and James up to go to school. While she scrambled eggs, I stared at her again, looking for evidence that she'd been eating bobby pins. But she just looked bored, pushing those eggs around the pan with a spatula. After breakfast I got ready to go to school.

I walked along behind James, lugging my red-plaid book satchel. The feeling from the dream kept rippling through my stomach, Rae beneath me, Mama hovering above us. All I could see was Mama chewing, her mouth full of copper-colored bobby pins. I wondered if the dream was a premonition. I had to do something. All of a sudden it was like a big torrent of water gushed out of nowhere and knocked me over, the water carrying me back down the hill toward our house. I ran as fast as I could, back to the house, back to Mama, my feet pounding the ground so hard my knees hurt. I ran up to the big sliding door on the back of our house and pressed my face to the cold glass, banging till my knuckles bruised.

Mama wasn't eating bobby pins. She was sitting at the kitchen table, talking on the telephone, her hair full of pink curlers, the receiver perched on her shoulder like a big black crow. She wouldn't let me in. She just looked at me, bobbing her head, and talked till she was finished, then got up and walked into her bedroom, glancing at me over her shoulder. I banged even louder, screaming "Mama," thinking she mustn't have seen me even though she'd looked right at me. Her face looked unsure, the way it had the day she let me drown.

In a minute she came back into the room and began washing the dishes, looking over at me every now and then with black eyes. I thought about throwing a rock through the glass the way I had at mine and Rae's shack, but it wouldn't make any difference; I'd still be locked out. She looked at me, but I knew she didn't see me and wasn't going to, either. I gave up and dropped to the ground and leaned against the door sobbing, even though I knew crying meant I was a sissy like James. I couldn't help it.

The radio was blaring. Maisey was home sick, still asleep. I stretched out my legs and closed my eyes. I guess Mama finally called Daddy home from work to come and take me to school, even though I could've just walked back by myself. He reached out his hand and pulled me up off the ground. "Let's go for a ride," he said.

As we walked to the car, I told Daddy what happened; he said Mama wouldn't let me in because she was afraid I'd wake Maisey up, but that's only because he hadn't seen her looking and not looking at me from behind the glass. I told him again, *She wouldn't let me in.* He pressed his lips together and nodded his head. I knew then that it hadn't happened. Daddy could make things disappear. Erase them.

He drove me uptown past the Dime Store, past Galloway's, then turned and headed toward the river. He drove slowly, as if he were taking me on a tour. Neither of us spoke. He was like a shadow, there and not there. The car bumped along on the sandy road, and when we came to the dam, he pulled in as if he was going to park, and let the car idle as I watched the water gushing through the locks. Then he backed up and turned the car toward town. He let me out in front of the school, and I walked down the dark halls, the smell of varnish heavy in the air.

When I walked home from school that afternoon, I felt my heart beating harder and harder the closer I got to our house. By the time I passed the pyracantha bushes and rounded the corner, I was so afraid that Mama wouldn't let me in the house that I wanted to jump into the azaleas and hide in the shadows beneath the green leaves. I was afraid she'd make me sit outside all night, and I wished and wished and wished I knew what to do so she'd let me in. Not knowing what to expect was like having a slingshot aimed at my face, the rubber band pulled tighter and tighter. But I figured out a way to forget scary or sad thoughts. After what happened to Rae, whenever I found myself remembering it, I said Peanut's magic word over and over again: *nine, nine, nine, nine, nine.*

I reached the door and slid it open. Mama stood by the ironing board, a pile of clothes on the table next to her. With her hand she moved the iron back and forth. Steam hissed out of it when she set it down to rearrange the shirt she was ironing. She looked up at me and smiled, said, "Hey, honey," as if nothing had happened.

16

That night while everybody else watched *Gunsmoke*, I
stole a cigarette from Daddy, got my bug jar, and snuck out
of the house. *To hell with being locked out*, I thought. *I'll give
Mama something to lock me out for.* I walked over to our
neighbor's property, a lot overgrown with kudzu. Only boys
were allowed to go out in the dark. And I felt like a boy, not
just any boy but Tarzan, sneaking through the jungle like a
panther. Pinpoints of light floated through the cool black air.
Slowly my eyes adjusted to the dark. I puffed on the cigarette
as I zigzagged through kudzu, peanut-butter jar in one hand,
the lid in the other, vines wrapping around my legs like a
thick green spiderweb.

As I ripped through the vines, I felt strong, like I could
do anything, go anywhere, without worrying. I took a deep
drag off the cigarette, felt dizzy. My bare feet dug into the
soft dirt, the damp crush of green. Lightning bugs blinked
and hovered over leaves; I imagined them as sparks of fire,
thought I could see green in all that darkness, the veins of
leaves. I flicked the cigarette into the weeds, then clapped
the lid over the jar, ripping the kudzu, capturing the

lightning bug, and ran quickly to catch another.

Later, Mama's frantic voice carried my name through the dark, *Lilywhereareyou*, and I heard it and didn't hear it; I was still Tarzan stalking the jungle. I caught one or two more bugs, then her voice sounded again, more insistent, *Lilycomehomenow*, and I decided not to hear her again. What could she do to me? Hit me? Leave me in a ditch? Lock me out for the rest of my life? She was no match for me. She could call my name all night.

I caught another lightning bug and was after another when I heard her shouting my name again. This time her voice cut though the air like a razor, prickling the hairs on my neck. I didn't hurry, though; if I was in trouble, I was in trouble. I'd take it like Tarzan would. She could burn me at the stake and I wouldn't flinch, not even when orange flames engulfed my body, blazed my hair.

I floated over the damp weeds as if I were already ash, drifting toward home slowly at first, cocky as the boy I had been. Then, for some reason, I panicked. I started to run. I knew I was in trouble. I raced to the house toward the yellow porch light. Mama met me at the door, barring my way in. Her red hair was twisted around pink foam curlers. Where her nightgown fell open at her neck, her skin was dusted white, sheeny with baby powder. Ugly brown moths swirled around my head as if it were on fire. I thought she was going to make me stay outside, but she didn't. Instead, she drew her hand back and slapped me so hard in the face that my ears rang. "Don't you ever go out of this house like that again," she screamed.

I guess I didn't look like I got it, because she went wild and started slapping me all over. I hunched my body over, clutching the jar to my chest while she slapped away, as if she were trying to put a fire out, screaming the whole time, her voice like a clenched fist, "I hate you I hate you I hate you."

Then Daddy appeared at the door behind her, Maisey and James behind him. He grabbed at Mama's arms, trying to push them down to her sides, while Maisey and James just stood there and watched. Daddy finally drug her away from me and I was left standing in the doorway, holding my jar, my body stinging, James and Maisey gaping at me like I was holding a gun.

Late that night I lay in bed staring at the dark. Maisey'd scootched as far away from me as she could, as if I had the plague or something. I could hear Mama and Daddy arguing above the sound of the TV in the other room, Mama's sharp barks followed by Daddy's soft murmurs. Their voices faded away as I watched the lightning bugs try to crawl out of their jar on the windowsill.

When they stopped blinking, I reached under my pillow and found the small cross Rae had given me one time to remember her by. It glowed in the dark. I snuck down the hall to the bathroom, closer to the sound of voices. As I lifted the paper cross up toward the dull yellow light, I heard Mama's voice: "She's going to send me over the edge, Dwayne. Something's wrong with that girl. She's just not normal."

I held my arm high. Daddy's voice replied, "Nothing's wrong....She's a tomboy....Leave her alone." I wondered what I'd done to make Mama think I wasn't normal. Maybe she'd found out that I'd broken the windows in mine and Rae's old house, or that I'd stolen James's underwear. I didn't want to be normal if it meant liking Barbie dolls or swimming in shallow water the rest of my life, but I didn't like being talked about either, so I murmured *nine nine nine nine nine* to myself, to shut the sound of their voices out.

17

When I was real little, Mama clutched me to her chest, mumbling I love you's into my ears. "You came straight from my heart," she sighed. She tumbled me over in her arms, gnawed on my neck, threatened to eat me alive. I shivered with pleasure, crying out, "Please don't eat me!" She growled.

Then she went to the hospital to get an operation to stop babies from ever coming again. When she came home, she gathered us around her bed as if to say, *I could've stopped you from coming, too.* I thought she was going to show us the place where the doctor cut her heart out. She raised her pale blue nightgown. I leaned forward to look, expecting a scar near her breast, where the doctor had reached in and scooped up her heart, the way Daddy scooped the guts out of fish. Instead, a red puckered line crisscrossed by stiff black stitches ran down her belly. A railroad track to nowhere.

Now just coming near us caused her head to throb. She came home from work, sat down in a chair, and dug that orange plastic bottle out of her purse. Shaking almost. She fumbled those pills to her mouth and swallowed them without water. When she went through one bottle, she'd get me or James to ride up to Rexall's with her and run in and get some more. "Come on," she said, "do this little favor for me." For a long time I did it, but one day it dawned on me that she never got the pills herself. The next time she asked me to ride uptown with her, I told I didn't want to anymore.

"Isn't there a law against kids buying drugs?" I asked. I thought the pharmacist, Mr. Keels, looked at me funny the last time I slid the bottle across the counter to him, like he was watching to see if I was going to steal something. He cupped the bottle in his hairy hand without even looking at it. Instead, he looked hard at me, like he had x-ray eyes. I didn't like it. When he turned away, I slipped a white pack of Wrigley's into my pocket.

"I have a refillable prescription, honey," Mama said and held out the bottle, pointing to where the doctor had typed "refill as needed."

"Then you go get them refilled; I don't want to anymore," I said. James didn't want to either and finally said he wouldn't. He didn't want Mama to be crazy, so she wasn't. *She's not crazy, she's not crazy, she's not crazy.* And he marched off to band practice in the middle of the night, sleepwalking, dragging his trumpet behind him. Not crazy. And he hit me in the head with a green croquet ball when I told him he was crazy like Mama for walking out of the house at night with his eyes wide open but asleep, always wanting everything to be perfect but it wasn't; we weren't perfect, and James hit me.

The morning after Mama slapped me for sneaking out, she came into my room and sat on the edge of my bed touching my shoulder softly. I knew I had a big bruise and I wanted her to look at it, the way it bloomed purple on my skin, the way she wanted us to look at those shiny specks of color on those butterflies. I wanted her to know just how bad she'd hurt me. I wanted her to remember that I hadn't cried. I wanted her to say, "I was wrong. You are the most wonderful girl in the world."

She patted the bed next to me. "Honey, come on. Get dressed and let's go for a ride," she said in a voice light as air. "I'll take you out to the River Road and let you drive." This was as close as I was going to get to an apology.

I knew I could get what I really wanted from her if I went along—she'd blossom into the mother who had nibbled my ears. I said okay.

I got up and dressed and she drove us out to the lake where we turned onto a red dirt road. She stopped the car and we both stepped out to switch places. Before I could slide into the driver's seat, Mama wrapped her arms around me from behind, hugged me so close I could hardly breathe. I let myself sink into her body for a moment; I smelled her skin, felt her breasts on my sore back.

"Ready?" she asked. I nodded, but I could've stood there all day.

She let me go and I climbed into the car, and she slid over next to me, propping her arm on my shoulder. As I drove, she gave me directions in her softest voice: *Watch out for that rock; oops, let's don't go in the ditch; get back on our side of the road.*

We passed Rae's house, and I tried to look at the yard without letting Mama know I was looking. Rae's rusted out bike lay in the grass, dandelions growing up through the spokes. I waited for her to say something nasty about Rae, but she didn't.

She let me drive for a long time. It was quiet except for the whispering of the tires over the sand. The creaking of the steering wheel. It was like I was in a movie and watching it at the same time. Even as I felt her body next to mine, I could see us as if from a distance, normal, a mother and daughter bumping down a dirt road in a car, sunlight ricocheting off the windshield, a big plume of red dust rising in the blue air behind us, then drifting down to settle on blackberry bushes as we passed.

It hadn't always been bad. There were beautiful days. The day Mama took us all to the Gulf of Mexico, where the water near the shore was green as glass. I wanted to swim way out where the water was deep, dark blue and dangerous but instead I sat on the bright white beach with Mama and Maisey, building castles. We were happy. Seagulls shrieked in the salty air above us. Mama scooped up handfuls of water and sand and dripped spires onto our castle walls. She made flags out of green seaweed and windows out of shells, told us to dig a moat and fill it with crocodiles. We did, but it couldn't keep the tide away. The castle dissolved in a surge of foamy water, a stream of sand washing away in the undertow.

Next Mama showed us how to make igloos and those were even better than castles because igloos are cold and we were sweltering beneath the hot yellow sun. Mama dug one brown foot into the powdery white sand, twisted her toes deep, then mounded more sand over her foot, patting hard. Slowly, she wiggled her foot out and there it was, an igloo on a beach in Florida. What struck me most, though, more than the icy white igloo, was the cool blue shadow Mama's body made on the beach when she stood to brush sand off her legs. I wanted to keep that cool blue shadow, that baby-blue mama, but when I reached my hand out to touch her, the light shifted and she was gone.

"Okay," she said, jarring me out of my dream. I stopped the car and opened the door to get out. She patted my leg, then slid over, slipping her hands over the steering wheel. I climbed into the passenger seat.

"That was fun, wasn't it?" she said. "We'll have to do it again soon." She took a deep breath, then cocked her head sideways and smiled at me, her eyes not soft anymore but hard and glittery. "Honey, I have a little favor to ask." She reached into her purse and pulled out the ugly orange bottle.

18

The next day Mama came home from work and went straight into her bedroom. She lay down without even taking her white uniform off. Dangled her feet over the edge of her bed, her white shoes still shining. When she laid across the bed diagonally like that, we all knew something was up. A migraine. A crying jag. She might even jump up and run into the kitchen and pull knives out of the drawers the way she did sometimes, threatening us. Like we were the enemies. I wondered why she didn't just get up and pop some pills.

Daddy came home from work, his rumpled khakis smelling of pesticide, and he looked down the hall to the bedroom and turned to us where we sat watching *Dark Shadows*. "Your mother not feeling well?" He didn't wait for us to answer but walked into the bedroom where she lay and changed into Bermuda shorts, still wearing his wingtips and black socks. When he came out, he started supper as if it was any other afternoon.

Mama didn't get out of bed for the next three days. Daddy made Maisey and I carry her glasses full of ginger ale, handfuls of saltines, food we ate when we were sick.

Mama wouldn't even look at us. We left the food on the table beside her bed, then picked it up and took it away a couple of hours later. It was like we were pretending to take care of her and she was pretending to be sick. She lay curled on her side like a snail, her eyes closed, the curtains drawn. Daddy knew something was wrong, but he didn't know what to do, so he told us to go get into his car. With a cigarette dangling off his lip, he said, "Let's get out of here. Let's go see the monkey." James got the front seat. Me and Maisey climbed into the back.

The monkey wasn't really our monkey, but we liked to think he was. He squatted in a metal cage on top of a pole down near the Apalachicola River, right out in front of Mackey's Tackle Shop. Licked his fingers. Scratched his fur. Stared at cars whizzing by. Who put him there? We didn't know. Daddy didn't, either.

On our way to see the monkey, we drove past the hospital. I saw Peanut standing next to a fence, rolling a cigarette. I waved at him, and he lifted his hand with six fingers and waved back. I spotted the Millers' beat-up Chevy gliding past Ruby's House of Hair. Mr. Miller drove, and Mrs. Miller sat scrunched over next to the window. As we drove past them, I twisted around to look out the rear window to see if Rae was sitting in the backseat. I couldn't tell.

Daddy didn't drive straight to the river, he drove away from it. We crossed into Georgia, kicked up red Georgia dirt, then crossed back into Florida again. "The monkey lives near a famous spot on the river," Daddy said, driving with one hand as he pulled a yellowed newspaper clipping out of his wallet and read it to us. "Ripley's Believe It or Not:

Near Chattahoochee it is possible to fish in two states, three rivers, four counties and two time zones at the same time."

Every five miles or so, Daddy remembered why we were out driving and said, in a voice like a Sunday preacher with a room full of sinners before him, "Y'all have got to be nicer to your mother." He said this looking straight ahead, as if he was afraid he'd wind up in the ditch if he looked at us, as if he knew he'd gotten it all wrong, that we weren't to blame, but he couldn't help himself. Whenever Mama got on a crying jag and laid across her bed, Daddy made us tiptoe into her dark room and whisper "I love you" in her ear to make her stop crying. It never worked, and I always walked out of her room feeling like a failure. I wanted to tell Daddy it was his fault. Mama didn't want us whispering in her ear; she didn't want us, period. She wanted a Cadillac. She wanted a vacation every summer; the kind of vacation those big, splashy billboards on Highway 27 offered: The Sunshine State! Shrimp dinners at Captain Anderson's! Watch the fleet come in! Pink-orange sunsets over a sea-green Gulf of Mexico!!! She's the one who wanted to be driven around looking at stupid stuff like monkeys. "If only I could go to Miami and see those blue-green parrots riding their little tricycles," she told us more than once, "I'd be one lucky woman." Her favorite color was aquamarine.

We drove over one rickety wooden bridge after another and Daddy stopped in the middle of them, even though we begged him not to. "Boring," we said. "Borrrr-ing." It was hot and humid. Even the bobwhites' "bob-white!" sounded slowed-down, like a record on the wrong speed. I knew then that Daddy was to blame for ruining Mama's Florida dream. One day she told him she wanted to drive south, hit all the major attractions: Parrot Jungle, Weeki Wachee, Marineland.

"Parrot Jungle is not Florida," Daddy had told her. "Those birds come from Africa."

His idea of a road trip was to ride down to Mackey's to see the monkey. When I pointed out that the monkey came from somewhere else, Daddy huffed, "That monkey was born in the backseat of Mackey's Delta 88. He's as native as you are."

"I want to show you something," Daddy said, while the car rocked to a halt in the middle of the bridge. "I want you to see something." And he ignored our groans, looked over our heads, out the window. "There's a beaver dam," he said. We looked. There was a pile of sticks in the creek. Every time Daddy saw a pile of wood in water, he thought a beaver chewed it up and put it there. He was always trying to show us stuff nobody else ever saw in real life. Alligator eggs, hummingbird nests, foxholes. "All in your own backyard," he said. I figured he was trying to prove something to us, and to Mama. He stared hard at the sticks like he was trying to memorize them, then tapped the gas and we rolled off the bridge.

He smoked one cigarette down to a hot orange nub, flipped it out the window, and lit another.

On the way to see the monkey, we saw eight snakes in eight different places, and Daddy didn't even try to run over them, even though every time James banged his hand against the side of the car, screaming, "Get him, Daddy, get him," and Maisey bounced up and down screaming, "Kill 'em, kill 'em, kill 'em." Daddy stopped the car and we hung out the windows watching the shiny black snake whip its body through the sand, into the ditch, and into the woods.

The monkey only lived about three miles from our house, but it took us two hours and two states to get there. Daddy drove us down gully-rutted red-clay roads that paled out and softened into powdery gray sand.

When he stopped the car so Maisey and I could pee, James jumped out the window and ran zigzag down the road, kicking up puffs of dirt, looking over his shoulder at us, laughing wildly. I squatted in sand up to my ankles, peeing, wondering out loud if we'd get stuck but Daddy said not to worry, the Fairlane was tough as a Sherman tank.

We got back in the car and Daddy muttered under his breath, "I ought to ride right past that damn James," but when we drove up next to him, Daddy hooked a thumb out the window like he was the one hitchhiking and growled, "Get in the car. Now."

Old refrigerators and washing machines rotted in dappled light under the scraggly pine trees that lined the road. "There was a patient that got stuck in one of those once," Daddy said, pointing at a rusty refrigerator turned over on its side. Spiky green palmettos grew all around it. "He's dead now, suff-o-cated." Our heads swiveled as we drove past it.

"That refrigerator?" Maisey asked. She knelt on the backseat so she could see it out the rear window.

"One of 'em," Daddy said.

"Why'd he climb inside a refrigerator?" James asked.

"Hiding," Daddy said. "He was running from the hospital, trying to escape those bloodhounds they put on his trail. He escaped them alright."

. . . . .

When we made it to Mackey's where the monkey lived, Daddy coasted the car to a stop. The monkey saw us and grabbed on to the thin metal bars with tiny pink fingers, like he was in jail. From the car, his gray eyes looked bigger than they were. When James walked over to the cage and leaned in close to talk to him, the monkey balled himself into a small gray lump, hunched his shoulders, folded his arms across his chest, and tucked his head down, eyes twitching. James bared his teeth, screeched monkey noises at him, monkey-dancing, flinging himself in circles, wheeling his arms as he twirled away.

Maisey and I broke butter cookies into pieces we called peanuts, then stood next to the cage, begging the monkey to eat them. We fed him; he didn't know the difference. When I leaned close to offer the monkey another cookie, I got a whiff of monkey pee.

Daddy slumped against the car smoking a cigarette. He looked tired. Droopy eyed and lost. He had black hair on his back and arms like the monkey, but he didn't have the monkey's charm. The monkey had watery gray eyes and human hands, tiny palms small as a stamp, pink fingers thin as matchsticks. He was our prisoner. We could do anything we wanted to with him.

When we ran out of cookies, we handed the monkey rocks, leaves, blades of grass. I handed him a crumpled cigarette butt, saying, "Here's a cookie, little monkey."

He sniffed it and Maisey laughed. "He's gonna eat it, look!"

We searched the ground for another cigarette butt to give

him. James speared a dried-up dog turd with a stick and tried to push it into the cage, but Daddy made him stop, corralling us all with both arms, whisper-yelling, "Get your asses in the car." Before I climbed in, I picked up a small rock and threw it at the cage. "Stupid animal," I said, as the rock pinged off the monkey's head.

"Jesus Christ, Lily," Daddy said. "Why'd you do that?"

I wanted to say *because that monkey has a nicer life than I do,* but before I could speak, Daddy said "Get your ass in the car." He took one last long drag off his cigarette, threw it smoking onto the ground, and stepped on it hard, twisting his foot as if he was trying to kill something.

On our way home, we drove Daddy crazy singing "99 Bottles of Beer on the Wall" and popping Bazooka like firecrackers in our mouths. When he turned red and leaned over the front seat, yelling and wagging at us his hand with its five fat fingers, threatening to beat us if we didn't stop singing, we fell all over each other laughing.

By the time we got home it was dark. Mama hadn't moved from the bed, but that didn't seem so bad since it was night.

When it was our turn to go to bed, I carried a tiny lamp my grandmother had given me. "Watch this," I said to Maisey as I turned the light on. A circle of light appeared on the ceiling. I held the lamp in one hand and made a shape with the other. A rabbit head popped out.

Maisey giggled. "Let me." She made a crocodile, then I made a duck, then she made a cat head. We took turns making animal heads on the ceiling. Then we tried to scare each other with how big they grew, their big gaping mouths, but the scariest I got was when I stopped looking at the giant dog I made and remembered Mama, Mama sleeping herself to death because I couldn't kiss her awake, and I just put my hand over the golden light, and my whole hand covered the ceiling. I looked at it; it wasn't mine, this big black hand. I made it even bigger, and it crept down the walls like a thundercloud descending, my whole hand covering the whole room. It wasn't until that moment that I let myself cry for all that had happened. I didn't want Maisey to see my tears, so I held the room in darkness until the lightbulb began to burn my palm, then turned it off and went to sleep.

19

She'd been threatening to have one as long as I knew her: when James sold our encyclopedias to the neighbors, when Maisey cut her bangs with pinking shears, when I rode my trike into the deep ditch across the street. It had gotten to the point that I thought you could choose to have a nervous breakdown, the way you chose pink shorts over yellow. The way I saw it, it was Mama's turn. Some mothers were supposed to have nervous breakdowns, the way Rae's mama had. Even though I couldn't imagine any of the other mothers I knew having one, I knew that Mama had been aiming for one for a long time.

It finally happened a few weeks after I started seventh grade. That morning, Mama was making breakfast and burnt the toast. The kitchen filled with a bitter black smell. James got mad and said, "Jesus, Mama, you always burn the toast; why do we always have to eat burnt toast?"

Normally she just scraped the burnt part off with a knife and gave it to us anyway, but this time she threw the toast and the knife into the sink, turned on us, and started screaming. "You try spending your life scrambling eggs, making toast, pouring milk, washing goddamn dishes, making beds, sweeping floors, washing clothes...." She stopped for a second to catch her breath. Her chin quivered the way Maisey's did whenever she was about to cry. Her eyes looked as if they had dissolved into water. "You try working and working and working and working for ungrateful children. You just try it."

She fell to her knees on the kitchen floor, dropping her head down, sobbing, her hands crawling through her hair, her whole body jerking the way a person jerks when they can't catch their breath and they can't stop crying, either. I wanted to throw my bowl of Rice Krispies into the garbage can; suddenly, the bowl felt like a weapon, and I was ashamed to be holding it. I sat it on the counter, reached out and touched Mama's back, her muscles hard as wood beneath the soft cotton gown. She tried to hit me, her spidery hands clawing at the air. I pulled back before she could touch me. None of us moved except to sway when she swayed, as if she were the water and we were the boats.

It was past 8:30 when James called Daddy at work to come home. Mama lay humped over on the floor, still as a pile of clothes. She wouldn't get up. We were late for school; then it was clear we weren't going at all.

When Daddy came home he squatted on the floor next to Mama, laid his hand on her back, said her name in his softest voice, "Katherine, Katherine." None of us moved. Daddy's face was gray with shadows. I don't think he could even see us. Somehow he got Mama to her feet and wrapped a blanket around her shoulders. She wouldn't even open her eyes, they were squeezed shut, and her mouth was a straight, washed-out line. Daddy told us to stay in the house while he took her to the doctor.

Maisey started crying as soon as they left. James turned on the TV and we sat down in front of it. I had this tickly feeling in my stomach, an in-between-laughing-and-crying feeling. As soon the picture flickered across the screen—a contestant spinning the Big Wheel while Bob Barker looked on—Maisey stopped whimpering and turned to me, "It's your fault, Lily. You're the one who always upsets Mama." She pooched her lips out. I wanted to hit her. The audience on TV screamed wildly.

"Yeah," James said. "You don't act normal. All my friends think you're a freak. You drive Mama nuts. If it weren't for you, Lily..." he started, but I'd had enough. I could hear my heart beating in my ears, I was so mad. But I half believed that what they were saying was true. How many times had Mama looked at me and said, "You are going to send me over the edge, drive me crazy, make me lose my marbles, cause me to have a nervous breakdown. You are going to make me stark-raving mad. You you you." Daddy had never really taken my side, either. How many times had he made me tell Mama I was sorry for driving her crazy when I hadn't even done anything?

I walked out of the house and flopped down in the front yard. The sky was a pale, pale blue. I decided I would lie in the grass all day. I concentrated on trying to make my heart stop beating, then James and Maisey would be sorry they said those things. They'd cry in the dark church at my funeral, think of the day they were mean to me. My absence would be like a loose tooth to them for the rest of their lives—they'd keep going back to it over and over, nudging it to go away, but it wouldn't. I'd haunt them *and* their stupid children.

My heart didn't slow down; in fact, it speeded up when I

thought of lying in a coffin, creepy organ music playing while my classmates filed by sneering at my body. *Look at her. She drove her mother crazy.* I wondered if Rae and Mrs. Miller would come to my funeral. Would Rae look at my lips and think, *Ooh, gross.* Would her mother begin a prayer over my body, then end by speaking in tongues and flopping around on the floor next to my coffin? The thought of Mrs. Miller's gibberish made me sit up. If I were going to have a funeral, I'd like to decide who could come and who couldn't.

. . . . .

Late that afternoon, we'd all wandered out to the front yard when Daddy drove up to the house with no Mama visible in the car. I thought maybe she was lying down in the backseat. But she wasn't. Daddy walked into the house and we followed him. Specks of burnt toast still dotted the edge of the sink in the kitchen. "Your mama's going to be away for a while," he said, hugging Maisey close to him, combing her brown, curly hair with his fingers. "It's like her head's a radio," he said, "except all her signals have gotten messed up. She's the same person she always was, though; we'll just have to be extra-careful with her when she comes home. She's like that old radio of James's—hit the knobs wrong and you foul the whole thing up."

"Is she going to the hospital here?" I asked. I didn't breathe for fear Daddy would say yes. I could just see Mama showing up at Unit 17 in a nightgown instead of her white uniform. And how horrible it would be if the seventh-graders went to sing to the patients while Mama sat there drooling and crossing her eyes, her nightgown twisted around her like a shroud. I knew I'd die for sure then. The whole town would know she was crazy.

"No, of course not," Daddy said. "The doctor is sending her to a small hospital in Tallahassee. She's not crazy; she's just tired."

I knew Daddy was just saying that. Mama was crazy and we all knew it. Everybody is tired, but not everybody would stand next to a lake and watch as a child nearly drowned. Still, I was relieved that she was going to a hospital in Tallahassee. This we could keep secret.

At first Daddy thought it best if we kids didn't go see her; "She needs a break from y'all," he said, and I wanted to say, *She's our mother and we made her crazy, so we can do anything we want with her.* But I didn't. I wondered what she would do all day. If she'd make tile ashtrays and little wood birdhouses like our patients did. Or would she sit in a dayroom in her nightgown and stare out the window? Or rock back and forth, slobbering, rubbing her hands? I wondered what the doctors were going to do to her. Were they going to give her a lobotomy so she'd be happy again? I wondered if she'd end up like Innertube, the patient who hung out at the gas station. He'd had a lobotomy. Maybe she'd get one too. Or maybe they'd zap her like they did Mrs. Miller.

A couple of weeks after she'd been gone, Daddy decided to take us over to see her. That old feeling of panic that had sent me running home from school to bang on the glass door washed over me as we headed down Highway 90 toward Tallahassee. Black shadows fell in stripes across the road, making me dizzy as we whipped past a stand of tall pines. Then we caught every red light in Quincy. All that starting and stopping made me carsick. I didn't want to see Mama; I wanted to go back home.

I didn't know what was worse, waiting for Mama to go crazy or knowing she'd finally done it.

The hospital seemed like a fortress to me, all white and straight up high. Tiny black windows like a hundred beady eyes. I didn't want to go in, and I don't think James or Maisey did, either, but Daddy pulled us all along. The air inside felt old, used-up. We passed a waiting room full of ordinary people and I relaxed a little. This was a regular hospital. The bell rang for the elevator. When the door joggled open, a man with a broken leg was pushed out by an orderly. The broken-legged man held a bouquet of yellow daisies on his lap.

The hall Mama was on smelled like a regular hospital, too: alcohol and Pine-Sol and cafeteria food smells swirled together. Mama glanced up when Daddy opened the door to her room. She didn't look crazy at first, just tired. She was sitting up in bed in a regular hospital room, eating cubes of red Jell-O out of a yellow plastic bowl. Her hair was flattened against the back of her head, and she had dark circles under her eyes, but she didn't seem to care. Then she spoke to Daddy: "And are these your children? My gosh, you've been busy, haven't you?"

None of us said a word. For a minute I thought she was playing a game with us, the way she'd done with Maisey and me when we were younger. She'd pretend not to see us even though we were huddled on the couch in full view. She'd walk around the room, looking for us, talking out loud to herself: "Where are my children? *Hmm*. I wonder if they went out to the blackberry patch. Oh lord, I wonder if a bear ate them." And then Maisey and I would squeal with laughter and pop up off the couch and beg her to do it again. Now Mama was simply gone. The face she had wasn't pretending. This face really didn't see us, really didn't know who we were. It hurt to look at her. When she rearranged her sheets I saw that she was wearing one of those ugly hospital gowns that open all down the back. Her hip stuck out and I could see the white of her bone beneath her dark skin. I wanted to cover it.

Daddy talked to her for a few moments, then backed us out of the room. It wasn't until later that I realized she had been zapped like Mrs. Miller had been and that she hadn't recognized Daddy, either. He'd decided to bring us over to see if our presence could jog her memory. Never mind that we were the cause of her breakdown. Never mind what effect seeing her would have on us. We were always being used one way or another. This time we were being used to gauge the treatment. Daddy told me later that he'd made the doctors stop the shock treatments after our visit. He said he'd rather have Mama crazy than lost in a haze.

Her being gone was hard; the house felt as if a big hole had been shot through it. Even though I knew it was silly, I almost expected Mama's voice when James turned on his radio to listen to a ball game. When I closed my eyes, I saw her with a radio head: knobs for eyes, a silver face pocked with holes, an antenna shooting out of the top of her head, radio waves zigging out of her ears at the speed of sound. I wondered if maybe we should get rid of all the radios in the house, maybe all the radios in the neighborhood; their shiny silver speakers and wandlike antennas spooked me. Everywhere I looked I saw radio waves shooting through the air like thin, black wires.

20

While Mama was in the hospital I was so lonely I got an overwhelming urge to see Rae, maybe because her mother had had a breakdown, maybe because something had broken between us and I wanted to see if I could fix it. I wanted to fix something. I couldn't leave well enough alone. Maybe I wanted to hold her in my arms again, pretend to be Harley Tucker so she'd let me kiss her. I wanted her to see me, not look past me as if I were invisible. I wanted her to say, "You were sweet to me, Lily, sweeter than that boy ever was." I wanted her to swing me in circles, to tap-dance across the dirty floor of our shack. I wanted her to laugh. I wanted us to be friends again.

I rode my bike past her house, hoping to get a glimpse of her in the yard or at the window. Nothing. Blazer stood at the back of the house, tethered to a tree with a frayed rope. I rode on past, thinking maybe Rae would be in our shack; I imagined myself saying I was sorry for breaking the windows, as if that was what had driven us apart. The shack was empty.

The next day, when I saw Rae in the hall at school I

practically tripped over myself to get next to her, to push myself through the crowd of kids so I could place myself where she'd have to say something just to get by me, but it didn't work. She walked right up to me and stood still, her lips pressed together, her eyes narrowed, until I moved out of her way to let her pass. In that moment I could see that the girl I'd kissed in the field was gone. Rae had grown taller than me; her white hair had darkened to a dull straw color. The white eyelashes I'd lingered over that day in the field were caked with greasy black mascara.

I couldn't understand how a person could change so quickly in one year, how she went from choosing me to choosing those boys. But I was kidding myself. After living with Mama, I should've been surprised if people didn't change as rapidly as wind. Hadn't my own Mama just gone crazy?

Once I realized that Rae wasn't going to see me, I decided to just let her go, to put her out of my mind, and to work on being normal so Mama would have a chance to be okay when she got home. At school I pretended to laugh at the boys' jokes. When the girls gathered in the bathroom to gossip, I acted interested. Partly I just wanted to make sure they weren't talking about me. I was afraid everyone would find out that Mama had had a nervous breakdown and was in the hospital, but no one seemed to know.

At home I swept the floors, washed dishes, washed and hung out clothes, took the clothes in and ironed them, all without being asked. I hoped that Daddy would tell Mama I was quite the young lady these days, hoped that would make her want to get well and come home.

. . . . .

When she finally came home a month after we'd gone to see her, she seemed fine, not tired but rested, like she'd just woken in a good mood from a long nap. She'd gotten most of her memory back and she recognized us, although I wondered if she really did or if Daddy had told her to fake it. I hugged her close to me that first night; she smelled like baby powder, the way she always smelled when she came into the bedroom to kiss Maisey and me good night. She treated our going to sleep as if we were babies going on a voyage; she nuzzled her mouth against my ears as if she might never see me again. When she kissed me, I listened as hard as I could to see if I could hear any radio music, maybe Johnny Cash or Merle Haggard, but I didn't, just the soft whoosh of her breath when she pulled away. There weren't any visible signs that she'd broken down, but I felt it. In some ways she was like a toy I'd smashed—now someone had fixed it and given it back to me. I was afraid of her.

Shortly after she got back, Mama woke us up one morning and said she'd missed us so much when she was gone that we could skip school that day. We stayed in bed longer and then piled into the car and drove uptown to the Dime Store. Before she got out of the car, she leaned over and looked at herself in the rearview mirror. She patted her hair, then clutched her purse. Maisey and James sat in the car while Mama and I went in to buy the kites. I wanted to see what she'd do; she never went into stores in Chattahoochee; she always made us go in places and buy things. I followed her into the store. I hadn't been in there in months. Mama walked down the aisles, looking for the box that held the kites and string. She picked up four of each.

We walked back to the front of the store. Mama laid the kites on the worn counter and sat her purse beside them. As Mrs. Bevis rang up the kites, she caught Mama's eye, then nodded over at me. "Home sick?" she asked.

Mama looked surprised. "Why, no," she said. "I'm not sick at all. I'm taking my children out to fly kites."

Mrs. Bevis raised her eyebrows, the way she used to raise them at Daddy when he brought me in to buy slingshots. I wanted to say, *She meant me, Mama,* but I was too scared to say anything, thinking I might give her away. I could tell Mama's being in this store was part of an act. She was trying to be normal.

"You know," Mama said. "I have spent entirely too much time indoors lately. And I bet you have, too." She glanced around the store. "It's awfully dark in here. Let me buy you a kite, and you come on and fly it with us. It's nice and sunny outside."

Mrs. Bevis laughed, then pushed the kites across the counter to Mama. "Honey, I got to work."

"Well, some other time," said Mama.

We drove back home and went into the house to get tails for the kites. Mama rummaged through the closets the way she did that day she took us butterfly hunting. She found a sheet and tore it into long, thin strips, and we tied knots into them. Then we unfurled the paper kites and put them together, attaching the tails. Looking at the brightly colored kites, I thought of the butterflies I had pinned into my cigar box, wondered if today was going to end in disaster.

She drove us to the field. She wore short shorts and she climbed out of the car and I expected her to say, "Just look at them and let them go," the way she had with the butterflies, but she didn't. She said, "Don't let go, don't let go of the string or your kite will fly away and we'll never catch it again."

I hadn't been in that field since the day I'd watched Rae with those boys. I'd stayed away from it, as if the place but not what had happened there was painful. Even though the memory had faded, as I walked over the grass, kite in my hand, I could still remember the warmth of Rae's breath on my cheek just before she kissed me; I could hear the boys' voices, talking her into walking off with them; I could see her lying in the grass, her legs bone-white against that blue sky. I felt my heart beating fast, the way it beat when I ran home that day, the way it beat later when I found out that Rae's mother had lost herself in the woods, had stopped talking, had gone crazy.

Our kites whipped high into the sky, and we held on to them, the wind washing over us like waves of water, and it was kind of like being underwater. The wind was blowing so hard. It was not easy to breathe, and I thought maybe Mama was trying to drown us in all this air, not just me this time. Maybe she thought we were babies who couldn't breathe in the wind.

Then, for some reason, all of the kites were loose and they were flying together in a bunch like butterflies skittering across the air. Mama ran after them, trying to catch the strings, but the strings were slithering across the ground like snakes and the kites were moving up and away from us and there was no way she could catch them. I ran after them; I ran toward them instead of away from them; I ran as if I could make up for the time I kept my butterflies and made Mama cry; I ran toward the edge of the field where Rae had

21

Me and James and Maisey stood on the carport next to a row of boxwoods arguing about who got the windows in our two-tone Fairlane and who got the front seat. Mama had been home for a month and we were going to Panama City Beach to try her out—see if she worked okay. Daddy said we should all act normal; there wasn't any sense in acting different. Life goes on, he said, you just have to go along with it. It was as if he was talking about a tornado, a flood, or a hurricane, something that would just sweep you away. Those were the kinds of things you just had to go along with.

Daddy lowered the ice chest into the trunk and we heard Mama talking to herself inside the house. "I don't want to go; I don't want to go. Don't make me go. Listen to them fight; they'll put me right back into the hospital."

I could see her sitting at the kitchen table, running her hands through her hair, tears streaking her face, her nose red and runny. Mama always did that. Every trip we ever took started with Mama not wanting to go, messed-up radio waves or not, unless it was her idea. And then something would go wrong anyway, like it did the day she took us out to fly kites.

Daddy patted his khakis to make sure he had the keys before slamming the trunk closed, then he yelled at us to shut up and walked back into the house, the screen door slapping shut behind him. James got his pocket-knife out and began carving his initials into the wooden cornerpost of the carport. Tiny wood shavings fell to the concrete slab. I sat on the porch steps and waited to see if maybe Daddy would come back out and get the ice chest. Maybe Mama was having another breakdown. Maisey sat beside me, sniffling and blubbering.

"She's gonna go," I said, "so stop being a baby." Maisey was eleven, but she still believed everything anybody said. She believed me and she believed Mama. She believed James when he stepped back from the pole, his silver knife glinting, and said, "I'm gonna cut this old wood pole in half and the roof's gonna come down and flatten the car." That started a whole new wave of tears.

James finished carving his initials into the pole, and Maisey stopped crying when Mama and Daddy walked out onto the porch. Mama's eyes were puffy and red, but she smiled at us, the way you smile when you want everyone to think you're okay. "Aren't y'all ready to go yet?" she asked.

"What are y'all waiting for?" Daddy said. "Get in the car, and no fighting about the windows."

Maisey jumped into the backseat next to a window, then me and James elbowed each other by the back door. He won; I had to sit in the middle, my feet on the hump, my knees jacked up in front of me. Daddy backed out of the driveway and we headed down Satsuma Street, windows down, our hair blowing in the wind. Motion calmed us; our anxiety fluttered out the window like scraps of paper.

Mama liked country music. At home she always tuned the radio to WSBP, a station stuck in the middle of a cow pasture just outside of River Junction. Her favorite song was "Honey" by Bobby Goldsboro. It was a slow sad song about a woman who died. Mama cried every time she heard the words "And honey I miss you, and I'm being good." Bobby Goldsboro's grandmother was a patient on Mama's ward. Mama gave Bobby Goldsboro's grandmother a bath once a week. She hoped Bobby Goldsboro would come to visit, but he never did. She still liked the song. When it came on the radio at home, she would stop ironing and sing along, tears running down her face onto the ironing board where they hissed when she ironed them away.

. . . . .

James rolled his eyes when Mama turned the radio on. "Why can't we ever listen to rock 'n' roll?" he said loudly to the whole car. He could never just let things be. Daddy shot him the evil eye in the rearview mirror.

Mama turned the radio up loud. The twangy music seemed to make her feel better. We reached the end of the street and Daddy turned onto Highway 20. Maisey leaned her head against the door and fell asleep. From the backseat, Mama and Daddy looked like girlfriend and boyfriend, Mama sitting close to Daddy. I imagined them holding hands, like they were in l-o-v-e, just riding in a car full of strangers, but both Daddy's hands gripped the wheel. His brown hair danced in the wind. Mama bobbed her head to the music.

I wanted us to be the way we used to be back when Mama was happy, but I wasn't sure when that was.

Heat rose off the pavement in dizzy waves of light. I looked over Mama's bony shoulders at the road narrowing in the distance. Way ahead, the pavement looked black and wet, but when we came to that part of the road, the slick black strip would disappear and the road would be dry.

When we'd been on the road for about an hour, James fell against me asleep, his mouth open, his brown eyes visible behind tiny slits in his eyelids.

For the next fifteen miles we were quiet, just listening to the wind and the radio. Then I saw the sign: Snake-a-torium, 5 miles.

Maisey leaned forward and tapped Daddy on the shoulder. "Let's stop at the Snake-a-torium."

Mama said it was too expensive, even though she didn't know how much it cost. I wondered how she ever expected to go to Cypress Gardens or Weeki Wachee. Did she think they'd let her in free? Maybe if she'd gotten the Miss Florida title they would've. But she didn't. This was her chance to see some real tourist attractions. Daddy was trying to give her something; this was better than the monkey by the river.

We passed another sign. *Snake-a-torium, Right Ahead.* Maisey tapped Daddy on the shoulder again. I leaned forward, looking out the window. James woke up.

"Stop, Daddy," Maisey said.

Daddy slowed down.

"Dwayne," Mama said. But Daddy was as bad as us. Once you put an idea into his head, he couldn't shake it. He coasted to the driveway, then swung the car into the gravel parking lot. The Snake-a-torium was a short white building. All along the front was a concrete-block wall with holes cut in it for decoration. Behind the wall were glass windows and behind those must have been cages filled with snakes. Daddy cut the car off and looked at Mama. "Let me just see how much it is."

When Daddy got out of the car, Mama turned around to look at us. She sighed loudly, then threw her arm over the back of her seat and patted my knee. "It wasn't any fun at first," she said, "you know, being in the hospital." She smiled and lowered her voice. "I felt like Frankenstein." She made a googly face to go with what she was saying. "After they zapped me a few times I felt better, almost like another person, except for feeling like I'd been kicked half to death by a mule. After that, though, we started having fun."

"You had fun?" I said, thinking of how it had been to see her at the hospital, to know that she didn't even recognize us.

"We went on field trips. Places children would go," Mama said, laughing. "They even took us to the Junior Museum. I hadn't been there since before Maisey was born. There I was with about ten other crazy people, wandering around the Junior Museum, looking at the pigs and cows and sheep like I'd never seen them before. I felt like Lucille Ball."

She acted like being crazy was her ticket to tour Florida the way she'd always wanted to. She'd gone to the Junior Museum and petted goats.

We sat in the car waiting for Daddy to come out. James opened his door and swung his legs out. Mama twisted the rearview mirror sideways and looked at her face. "Y'all know we can't afford to go in there. You can see snakes for free." I hated her for saying that, even though it was true, and glared at the back of her head. She caught my eye in the mirror and held it. I felt like she was trying to pull me out of myself, draw me inside her like a breath. I looked away.

Daddy came out of the Snake-a-torium shaking his head. He leaned into the window. "It's too much, gang. A buck fifty a pop. You won't be able to ride the roller coaster if we go in here."

We got out of the car anyway. James stood up and stretched. Maisey opened her door and got out. I climbed out of the car and followed James up next to the building. We all put our hands on the white concrete blocks.

"Hear 'em?" Maisey whispered, her eyes wide. She dropped her hands and stepped back. Daddy leaned against the car smoking a cigarette and watching us.

"I hear 'em," James said, making a rattling sound with his tongue.

I listened. Faint rattling sounds came from inside the building, or maybe it was the leaves rustling in the pecan trees next to the parking lot. I put my ear against the concrete block. It was like putting a seashell next to my ear to hear the ocean. I heard all sorts of sounds—slithering, rustling, rattling. I could see the snakes curled up in their cages, coiled to strike.

"I hear a diamondback rattler," Maisey said. "He must be seven feet long."

"Come on," Mama hollered from the car. "Let's get out of here. It's hot as hell." She fanned her face with her hand.

We piled back into the car and pulled off, the gravel snapping, the wind hissing as Daddy accelerated down the highway.

. . . . .

Daddy drove down the oyster-shell drive to the Bid-a-Wee cabin. There were three small bedrooms and a yard filled with straggly grass and sandspurs. Even though the cabin was a block away from the beach, you could sit on the porch and hear the waves rolling in.

We unpacked the car, and Mama and Daddy went in to the kitchen and started making baloney sandwiches. Nobody wanted one because if we ate them, Mama would make us wait an hour or two before putting on our swimsuits. Me and James ran outside and Maisey sat on the porch listening to the waves. The first thing I did was step on a sandspur, and when I bent over to pull it out of my foot, I spotted some lizards crawling in the bushes next to the cottage. I got an idea. I caught one of the lizards and held it next to my ear. It bit down and hung on. I scooped up another one and stuck it on to my other ear. I laughed out loud, thinking how funny I must've looked. I walked slowly onto the porch, the green lizards dangling from my earlobes like earrings. Maisey screamed and Mama and Daddy ran out onto the porch.

A year ago Mama would've thought I was funny. She was the one who made up stories about lizards carrying pennies in their throats; she was the one who made up stories about why their tails broke off when you tried to catch them. Now she was a lizard, changing colors every five feet.

"My God," Mama said. "Get out of here and get those damn things off of you." I stood there smiling, thinking she would see how funny I was in just a minute. The lizards' long green bodies hung limp as weeds against my cheeks.

"Get out," Mama screamed.

"Go on," Daddy said, "you heard her."

I turned carefully so the lizards wouldn't fall, but one of them dropped to the cool concrete slab and ran toward Maisey. She jumped on top of the wicker chair she'd been sitting in and her foot punched right through and she scratched her leg. Mama ran after me, smacking me so hard on the back of the head that the other lizard flew across the porch and landed on the screen, a black silhouette. When I stopped to rub my head, she slapped me hard in the face.

James ran onto the porch, scooped the lizard into his hands, and carried him out. Mama and Maisey both started crying. "I want to go home," Mama said. Daddy circled her with his arms the way you're supposed to hold someone in water when you're saving them from drowning. Part of me wanted him to let her go; another part of me wanted to save her myself. They floated away from us.

James walked back onto the porch, flashing his palms at us. "The lizard's gone," he said calmly. "Everything's going to be all right, Mama. Please stop crying."

Maisey rubbed her leg; a thin line of blood beaded on her skin like stitches in cloth. "I'm okay, Mama. I was scared."

"Let's don't go home," I said. "I didn't mean to hurt anybody."

"You're always saying that," James said. "Why don't you just stop acting stupid?"

"Let's go inside and eat like normal people," Daddy said.

Mama calmed down after we ate, but she wouldn't let us go near the beach, so Daddy decided to take us all for a ride down the Strip. We had to keep moving if we were going to stay normal. We were like tops spinning across a table; when we slowed down we got wobbly, dangerously close to each other.

Daddy drove up to Alvin's Beach Memories, a souvenir shop. I didn't get excited because we never bought anything; we just walked through the air-conditioned store, the air musical with wind chimes, and we played with everything like we were at somebody else's house. When we walked into the store, Daddy put on a sailor hat and a pair of yellow Mickey Mouse sunglasses and wobbled back and forth like a bear. Maisey and I traipsed around as if we owned the place; I looked at dead baby sharks bobbing in jars of blue formaldehyde, their tiny, white teeth set in jagged grins. Maisey slapped around on flip-flops decorated with red plastic flowers while James raced down the aisles with a green plastic alligator. Mama unfurled a beach towel with a map of Florida printed on it, snapping it like a flag, and Daddy fingered an air plant growing out of a conch shell like whiskers.

Off in a corner of the store I found a toy hula dancer. I looked around to see if anyone was watching, and pulled her out of the box. She wore a real grass skirt. When I squeezed her belly, her lime-green bathing suit top flipped down and her titties popped out like balloons with pointy red nipples. I laughed to myself. I squeezed the hula dancer over and over and over, until I heard Mama calling my name. Her voice grew closer and closer. There was no way I could get the dancer back into the box before she caught me, so I quickly stuffed her into my shorts.

Mama stood before me. "Come on," she said. "What were you looking at?"

My eyes went right to the empty hula dancer's box. "Nothing," I said. "Did you find anything you wanted?" I pressed my hand against my belly as we walked down the aisle to make sure the hula dancer didn't fall out. In my head I was praying *Please, God, don't let me get caught.* I didn't breathe until I walked outside and climbed back into the hot car, the hula dancer digging into my belly.

Daddy pulled onto the Strip, the Fairlane chugging along in traffic, a plaster duck in a shooting gallery. We passed the amusement park, the wooden roller coaster, the Spider, the Tilt-a-Wheel, the Ring of Fire, all whirring and spinning like the inside of a clock.

We drove past Goofy Golf, the big plaster dinosaurs and Kon-Tiki men towering over the car and headed out toward St. Joseph's Bay. We were near the bay bridge when James saw the sign: Boat Rides: $3. A red arrow pointed to a small wooden shed next to a dock that jutted out into the bay. Little wooden boats with motors bobbed in the brownish-colored water. Brightly colored sailboats skimmed the water like kites.

"Daddy, stop," James shouted. "Let's go there."

Mama and Daddy swiveled their heads to the left. It looked like something we could all do.

"Three dollars, Katherine," Daddy said to Mama. "Why not? The kids haven't done anything that cost money all day." He flicked the blinker on and when there was a lull in traffic glided the Fairlane down the oyster-shell road into the sandy parking lot. James swung his door open before the car even stopped. We scrambled out of the car, ready for our first real adventure of the day. I'd never been on a boat and could see myself zooming around the bay, the throttle wide open.

We ran up to the gate and stepped inside the shack. An old man stood behind a counter at the far end, selling tickets and giving instructions to a man and a little girl. People leaned over tables piled high with dried-out shark jaws, shells, and T-shirts.

"Oh no," Mama groaned. She pointed to a sign hanging above the counter where the old man sat drinking a coke. The man and the little girl walked outside and got into one of the boats anchored at the dock.

"Three dollars per person," Mama read out loud. "I thought all of us could go for three dollars."

"Let me go." James said, "I've never been on a boat."

"I want to go," I said. "I never get to do anything. I'd rather do this than go to the stupid Miracle Strip."

"Please, please, please," James said, tugging Daddy's arm.

Maisey started in. "I wanna go."

"Would y'all please, please, please, please, please, please, please be quiet," Mama said. Her face was tight. We all knew what that meant. *Please, please, please.*

Daddy took a long, deep breath. "Christ," he said. "Can't we ever go anywhere?" He looked away from us. For a couple of seconds we all kind of stared at the dirt. "You kids are just going to have to deal with it. It costs too much," he said in a tired voice.

James screamed, "I hate you, I hate you," and turned away from Daddy.

Maisey held Mama's hand. "Let's me and you go, Mama. I've got fifty cents."

Mama bit her lip; tears welled up in her eyes. People stopped looking at the shark jaws and started looking at us. The old man watched. Past the door, I could see the man and the little girl steering their boat out to the middle of the bay, water rippling behind them.

"Dwayne, I can't stand this," Mama said. Her voice had a trembly sound, like a radio station losing its signal. James looked up at Mama and out at the wooden boats shifting side to side in the water. He stepped toward the old man; I could see what he was thinking. If he could just get through the door he could steer the boat, and when he came back everything would be okay.

"Wait a minute, James," Daddy said. "Christ. Christ. What in the hell is this? All this damn fighting. What the hell's going on? What is this?"

Nobody said anything.

"Go sit on that bench over there." He waved his hand at us. "All of you. And I don't want to hear a word out of a one of you, not a word. Not for the rest of the day. Your mama and I are going out on one of those boats and I want y'all to be quiet by the time we get back."

"Come on, honey; it'll be me and you, just like old times. Let's get on that boat. Come on." He took her by the arm and guided her across the dirt floor to the ticket booth. Tears ran down her face. Daddy fished the money out of his pocket, paid the man, and walked Mama out the screen door and onto the dock toward a blue boat. At least I had the hula dancer. I pulled her out of my shorts and held her close so no one would see her.

Maisey swung her legs back and forth and James covered his face with his hands. I watched Daddy help Mama into the boat, one slender leg after the other. She sat down and Daddy put the orange life jacket over her head, careful not to look in our direction. Mama wiped her tears with the back of her hand and Daddy put on his life jacket and started the motor. They pulled away from the dock, just the two of them.

22

After our beach trip, Mama started feeling bad again and got it in her head that changing her hair color would change her mind, make her happy. "To hell with these pills," she said, tossing a bottle of lithium into the trash can. She stood in my bedroom, holding a wide glass jar of Dippity-Do up to the light, looking at the bubbles in the green gel. "Your hair can determine your personality," she said, wagging the jar at me. "If you don't believe me, come to the hospital sometime. The ladies who get their hair done each week are not as crazy as the ones who just sit there with a rat's nest perched on top of their heads." She set the jar of Dippity-Do down on my dresser. "It's order, Lily, and what better place to start than with the hair on your head? Let me tell you," she said, "being a redhead has brought me nothing but trouble. People take one look at my hair and expect me to misbehave, and then I can't disappoint them."

She'd experimented with her hair before. She went through the wig stage before she'd had a nervous breakdown. At the height of it, she had about ten different wigs, of all cuts and colors, from black wigs that flipped at the ends to blond shags, to brown ones that frizzed out like poodle hair. I had to admit that the wigs did seem to have a certain power. Daddy put a blond wig on at the beach once, and he climbed on top of the picnic table and did a hula dance.

At the end of the wig period, James painted scary faces on Mama's styrofoam wig heads, then hid them in the utility room off the carport, where both the wigs and the heads were slowly being eaten by roaches.

Almost every other woman in Chattahoochee had gone through that phase, too—women with straight hair wore curly wigs, women with curly hair wore straight wigs, black women wore blond wigs. Women who didn't want to go all the way wore falls, long pieces of blond or black or red hair they pinned onto the backs of their heads like horsetails.

Mama said wearing a curly wig had made her feel spunky. "So imagine," she said, "imagine what changing my actual hair color will do. Look what it does for MayBelle Carr," she said. And Mama was right. MayBelle Carr dyed her hair jet-black and drove around town in a long gray Eldorado. She was about a hundred and fifty years old. Once a couple of patients had escaped and tied her to a chair and stolen her Eldorado, but not before they asked her to come on and go with them. "You sho' are a good-looking woman," they told her. "What are you? Twenty-eight, thirty?" She told everyone the escapees were perfect gentlemen; if they hadn't been wearing pajamas, she might've gone along, they were so polite.

Mama went up to the Dollar Store and bought ten different colors of hair dye, everything from Midnight Black to Sassy Blond. Then the next weekend when Daddy and

Maisey went to Tallahassee, Mama decided to let me and James help her dye her hair to surprise him when he came back. "Let's see," she said, looking into the medicine cabinet, where she kept all the hair dye. "What color do we want to go with? *Hmm.*"

She picked one of the brunettes because she liked Jackie Kennedy. We went into the kitchen so we could use the sink, and James and I knelt on chairs on either side of Mama. We poured the dye into her hair and rubbed it in. After twenty minutes or so, she rinsed, then dried off with a towel. "Let's take a Polaroid of it with Maisey's Big Shot," Mama said, "so I can see how it'll look." She put her hands on her hips. Smiled at the camera. Brownish-colored water ran down the back of her neck. James took the shot and Mama studied it as it developed, holding the picture up close and then far away. She decided she didn't like that color—it made her look mousy, she said—and she decided to try the blackest black, the Cleopatra Black. She leaned back over the sink while James and I kneeled again on either side of her, rubbing the color into her hair.

When we were done, she dried her hair, then cocked her head to one side and smiled while James took another Polaroid, but she didn't like the black, either. "It's really too, too much like Cleopatra," she said, so she decided to bleach it out. Something happened, though, with the peroxide and the dye. When she poured the peroxide over her hair, instead of bleaching it white, it splotched her hair all up—like fake leopard fur. She stared at herself in the mirror and her face crumpled and she started crying. I thought, *Oh no, here we go. Back to the hospital.*

"James," she said, "we might as well get a shot of this, too."

I couldn't believe she was handling it, but there she was. She leaned back against the kitchen sink. James snapped the photo, and we all watched as her image slowly developed. She wasn't smiling anymore. "Well," she said, matter-of-factly, tossing the photograph onto the kitchen counter, "it'll have to come off. Lily, get me the scissors; they're in your brother's room."

I didn't think she would really cut her hair, but I got the scissors anyway. She took them from me, held them in her hand for a moment, a strange look on her face, then grabbed up a thick hank of hair and cut it off. She dropped the snaky wet locks onto the floor. I couldn't believe she actually did it. Then she went into the bathroom, picked up Daddy's razor and his Barbasol, and lathered what was left. James and I stood in the doorway and watched while she shaved her head right down to the scalp. Then I took another picture of her frowning, a fleck of white foam on her left eyebrow.

When Daddy and Maisey came home, Daddy took one look at Mama sitting on the couch, her bald head wrapped in the scarf she would wear for the next six months, and all he said was, "You're just one big surprise after another, aren't you?"

And she was. As soon as her hair grew back late that summer, she dyed it platinum blond. The very next day Maisey and I went to the Baptist church camp for a week. When Mama and Daddy drove us up to the church to get on the raggedy church bus, Mama wouldn't budge out of the car. I stood sweating in the hot morning sun watching Cindy Glisson and Betty Jo Benefield hug their mothers good-bye, body to body. Embarrassed, I bent through the passenger window to peck Mama on the cheek. Then Maisey and I stood next to our suitcases and waited for someone to tell us to get on the bus.

It was a miserable week. The first night I slept on the bottom bunk, terrified the girl on top would fall and crush me. When I drifted off to sleep, I dreamed of my mother's face, surrounded by platinum curls. *Who's that? That's my mother.* It was weird having a mother who changed her hair color the way some people change clothes.

The next morning, a chubby girl named Cassandra woke up everybody in the cabin, shouting at our counselor, a shy seventeen-year-old girl named Lissette. "I bet you've never had an orgasm," Cassandra shouted. She pushed herself up in bed and ran her fingers through her rumpled brown hair.

I leaned over to see what was happening. The cabin was dark and damp and smelled like mold. Lissette folded her arms over her chest. Her long blond hair was pulled back in a ponytail. "Would you be quiet?" she whispered loudly. "You're waking everyone up."

"I bet you don't even know what a clit is," Cassandra said, throwing the covers back, climbing out of her bed. Her short, yellow gown was hiked up around her thick thighs. "I bet you you're a *ho-mo-sex-u-al*. You're going to end up being a dried-up old maid. You probably don't even know what an orgasm is."

I didn't, and from the looks on the faces of the girls sitting up in their bunk beds, they didn't, either. We were all awake at this point. A couple of the girls were crying. Lissette stormed out of the cabin while Cassandra hollered after her, spitting out the words "queer, queer, queer." She turned to look at the rest of us in our bunks. "She's a lezzie," she said, putting her hands on her hips as if that were that.

By lunchtime, rumor had it that Lissette had caught Cassandra playing with herself and asked her to stop. That's when Cassandra blew up. I still wasn't sure what an orgasm was, but that's not what bothered me or anyone else. What grossed everyone out, what made the girls cry and titter nervously, was the word "lesbian." I knew what a lesbian was. I was reading Ann Landers once and saw a letter about homosexuals, and I looked the word up in the dictionary. Someone who is attracted to the same sex, it said.

Lissette got Cassandra moved to another cabin, but the rest of the week, in between Bible study and vespers, all anyone talked about was queers. We sat next to the lake where velvety brown cattails rustled in the wind and discussed all the ways you could tell if a girl wasn't normal: if she had short hair, if she carried her books by her side instead of up against her chest, if she turned her hand around to look at her fingernails instead of holding her hand out flat. Queers had their own ways of standing or walking across rooms. Girl queers played softball; boy queers played piano or took up ballet. Boy queers lisped and stuck their pinkies out, and girl queers sat with their legs wide apart. By the end of camp, I was afraid I'd sit down the wrong way. I kept reminding myself to cross my legs, and I had to remember to hold my Bible against my chest when we walked to vespers at sundown. I knew I'd be in deep trouble if anyone ever found out that I hated wearing dresses, that I'd kissed Rae, or that I'd stood in a souvenir store looking at a doll's titties.

For once, I couldn't wait to go home.

When Maisey and I arrived home at the end of the week, I half expected Mama to be a redhead again. I got our bags off the bus and Maisey and I walked toward the Fairlane. I was careful to carry my bag the same way the other girls carried theirs. The windshield was glazed with sunlight, so I couldn't see in.

"I got a surprise for you," Mama said when I climbed into the car. Her hair was still blond. She was sitting right next to Daddy, holding his hand. Maybe blondes did have more fun.

She had redecorated our bedroom. When we got home, she led us to the doorway, then stepped aside so we could look in. One wall was Elmer-glued with cloth she must've picked up at the bargain bin in the Dollar General. Pulsating red polka dots outlined in black and white, with lots of little dots in between. The pattern made my eyes swizzle. Maisey and I sat on a bedspread made out of the same material, bobbing our heads up and down at Mama as she stood in the doorway to our room. "Do you like it? Don't you just love it? I think it's kind of psychedelic." She sat down next to us on the bed. "At the hospital, they always talked about how important your surroundings are. 'You're a product of your environment,' they said. So I thought this would spunk you girls up."

23

I don't know whether or not it was the psychedelic cloth on the walls, but after I came back from camp, I decided to be different, not like Mama when she changed her hair color, but really different. *I knew* I had to get it together. I realized that what Mama had said about me all along was true—something was wrong with me. Mama had always seen it, and after camp, I was sure other people could see it, too. I didn't feel like I belonged anywhere. So I decided to fall in love with Ronnie Lubjek the day I met him. I needed to be normal.

We were both fourteen then; he had just moved to Chattahoochee with his mother. Nobody I knew had moved to Chattahoochee since Rae, but she didn't count because her mama went crazy. People just didn't move to Chattahoochee to start a life—you had to be born here or be crazy enough to get sent to the hospital—so Mama dragged me over to meet the Lubjeks. It was her big chance to be normal, too, to do one of those Welcome Wagon things she read about in some magazine while sitting in her psychiatrist's office— muffins or cupcakes or flowers; I don't remember, but she was inspired. Mama wouldn't let people in our house, and we never brought friends over either, but she was always making things for the people we came in contact with, especially teachers: shellacked purses were in for a while, then burlap, then those pictures of roosters made from fifty zillion different kinds of seeds. I was still finding poppy seeds and lentils from the last time she glued one of those birds together.

I hadn't had a crush on anyone since Rae, but I told myself that didn't count because she was a girl and nothing ever happened between us. My memory of her had faded until all that was left was an image of her white legs. I told myself she'd wanted to kiss me and I let her even though I had to pretend to be a boy. Whenever I thought of what happened in that field with those boys, I felt a sharp ache in my chest. I blocked it out as much as I could.

When I got to eighth grade, I started hanging out with Betty Colson, a thin girl with wispy, black hair. We sat next to each other in band. I thought she was lucky because she lived in a house on the hospital grounds, right next to a building patients lived in. Living there meant her parents didn't have to pay rent, so they had more money. Creditors didn't call her Daddy the way they called mine.

After school some days, we walked down to the Jr. Food store to buy *True Romance* comics. Love was drawn in black-and-white between the slick covers of those babies: *Teen Confessions, My Love Diary, My Secret Desire*; you just had to fit inside the lines. There was always a handsome man, and he was always mysterious, distant, and exotic, and Ronnie was about as exotic as Chattahoochee ever got. His father was dead. He lived with his mother. He had bright carrot-colored hair and freckles. He sat at the kitchen table looking out the window, a spoon in his hand. As I stood looking at him, a flat black-and-white movie flicked on and off behind my eyelids. Me and Ronnie. Me and Ronnie. Finding a boy and falling in love was what I was supposed to do, and I finally knew it, even though at school, when the eighth-grade girls gathered in the bathroom to smoke and talk about their boyfriends, I leaned against the green-tiled wall, bored, inhaling deeply, letting the blue smoke drift out of my nose. I never said a word about Ronnie. I thought about how stupid those girls were. I hated the way they ringed their eyes with black mascara, the way they smeared their eyelids blue or green like bruises. I hated their cherry-red lips and the way they all hung out at night under the oily streetlights at the Chattaburger uptown, sitting on the still-warm hoods of fast cars that would never take them anywhere.

I fell in love with Ronnie's mother first. Mama forgot to tell me Mrs. Lubjek was deaf, so when we got up to the apartment, after clanking up the stairs like insurance salesmen, I thought she was from a foreign country. She spoke with a thick accent, stumbling across a word here and there. "Look at by fase," Mrs. Lubjek said to me, smiling as she took the muffins Mama held out to her. "Look at by fase so I cad read your libs. I'b deaf you know. I cand hear you."

I couldn't take my eyes off of her; she didn't look like any of the mothers I knew—she was gorgeous. Wavy brown hair and soft green eyes that took me right in. It was love at first sight, although I wouldn't have called it that. She was, after all, somebody's mother. When she turned her head for a second to look at Ronnie, Mama whispered at me loudly, "Stop staring." I wondered why Mrs. Lubjek didn't use sign language—I'd seen deaf people on TV, fluttering their hands at each other like bird's wings. Ronnie told me later that his mother didn't want to be more different than she already was. She wanted to fit in, which was kind of funny since she didn't have a car or a husband.

Ronnie's deaf mother was even better than him being from Someplace Else; she was from another world, a world where words are silent shapes in the air. Words probably felt like LifeSavers in her mouth, 3-D, how you feel for the hole with your tongue. She was a magician turning air into sound that she couldn't even hear, reading words right off our lips like a spy. I could've lain on the wooden floor the whole afternoon watching her speak, watching her read words off Mama's mouth. Ronnie sat at the kitchen table eating cereal like nothing special was happening.

Standing in that garage apartment, I knew that carrot-topped Ronnie Lubjek got up in the middle of the night while his mother slept and turned the black-and-white TV on. I stared at him while Mama spoke to Mrs. Lubjek stupidly, as if she were speaking to a two-year-old, and I imagined Ronnie lying on the dusty wood floor in front of the black and white TV watching *X Minus One* or one of those Godzilla movies that came on after midnight, the sound turned up as loud as it would go, the pale gray light washing over the walls, the ceiling, the windows, Ronnie Lubjek's dark brown eyes. I could do this.

24

Nobody ever dropped by our house to see Mama and Daddy, except for relatives on their way somewhere else every now and then, and it was a good thing, because you never knew what Mama would be up to. Since she threw away the pills the doctor had prescribed for her breakdown, she'd gotten crazier than ever. She might waltz around the house in one of her old party dresses, the zipper undone down the back because the dress didn't fit her anymore, or she might say, "Goddamn, you got a big nose," or something even worse. Sometimes she just didn't care what people thought. Once one of my teachers came down to the house and Mama wouldn't even come out of the bedroom to meet her. Try explaining that. But then sometimes she did care. When Aunt Ola, one of Daddy's sisters, called and asked if she could stay with us on her way to Miami, Mama made Daddy go out and buy a new couch so Ola wouldn't think we were trash.

After our visit to Mrs. Lubjek, we never went anywhere to see anybody. Mama and Daddy didn't have any friends, except for people they worked with. So it was a big deal when this couple named Bobby and Barbara—just like the singing and dancing couple on Lawrence Welk—invited us all over to their house in Sneads for a barbeque.

Bobby worked in Mama's building; I'd seen him before when I rode with Daddy to pick Mama up; he was a dark-skinned man with thick black hair that he slicked back with butch wax. Every time I saw him he was wearing tight blue jeans and a belt with a silver buckle the size of an ashtray. I figured he lived in a trailer out in the middle of a horse pasture, but he didn't.

Daddy drove over the bridge into Sneads, then turned left at Buddy's Vegetable stand and drove another couple of blocks crouched forward in his seat, looking for the Carters' house. All the houses looked the same to me. Red brick. White trim. The basic box.

"There it is!" Mama said, pointing at one of the houses. Daddy pulled into the carport behind an old green pickup truck.

The Carters lived in a halfway-decent house, but the yard was ratty with weeds. A lawn mower sat right in the middle of it at the end of a mowed strip. Barbara opened the door when we drove up; she was tall and thin, her bleached-blond hair black at the roots. Their thirteen-year-old, Troy, scooted out past her. He had a big head and looked like Alfred E. Newman, the kid on the cover of *Mad* magazine. He stood on the edge of the carport, arms crossed, watching as we got out of the car, staring at us as if we were aliens.

Bobby and Barbara had blue everything. Their couch was blue; the walls were blue; the shag carpet was blue; the La-Z-Boy was blue. What wasn't blue was black. The starburst clock. Ashtrays as big as plates. The porcelain Siamese Cat sitting on the smoked-glass end table. The house was one big bruise. Me and James and Maisey crowded down the hall into Troy's bedroom, but there was nowhere to stand. The floor was covered with plastic horses, GI Joes, a basketball, a football, a cap gun, Monopoly money, bird feathers, a Halloween mask, dirty blue jeans and t-shirts. Mama would've died if she'd seen all that. An unmade bed gave her the shivers. But Daddy and her had settled onto the couch in the black-and-blue living room.

Since we couldn't all fit into Troy's bedroom, we moseyed back down the hall to the living room. Bobby had just dug a can of Budweiser out of the icebox and held it out to Daddy. I wasn't surprised that Bobby and Barbara drank, since they lived in Jackson County, which was "wet," which meant you could buy liquor there, which you couldn't in Gadsden County, where we lived. The Baptists just wouldn't have it.

Daddy raised his hand toward the beer; I just knew he was going to make a stop sign like a cop in traffic, but he didn't. He clamped his hand onto that can of beer as if he'd been drinking his whole life. It hissed when he popped it open. Then he glanced over at us kids and told us to go on outside and play, like he was showing off or something. He never talked to us like that at home. Well, I thought, Daddy drinking that beer would send Mama over the edge. Even though she still had her bottle of Darvon, she was dead set against alcohol; she helped Maisey make a poster for school once, showing the evils of liquor. She cut a picture of a bottle of Four Roses Bourbon out of a magazine and pasted it onto a picture of an open casket. Then she pasted one rose in each corner. She believed liquor would kill you. Well, she surprised us. We were filing out of the house when Bobby fished another beer out of the icebox. I looked over my shoulder just in time to see Mama lift her hand and take it.

None of us said anything about the beer, maybe because we didn't want Troy to think anything strange was happening, or maybe because we didn't want to hurt his feelings. We hung out in the front yard for what seemed like hours. We climbed the stringy mimosa tree, played hide-and-seek, and ran races down the middle of the street, boys against girls. We were sweaty when Bobby called us into the backyard, where he was barbequing next to a withered up dogwood tree. Daddy stood next to the grill with Bobby, holding an empty platter in his hands. I looked to see if Mama had a beer and she did. She sat next to Barbara on an aluminum beach chair that was tilted to one side. She had a strange look on her face, too, as if she was thinking of something funny, trying not to laugh. When she wasn't looking, James picked up an empty beer can and pretended to chug it down. Maisey and I acted like nothing was out of the ordinary. When we finished eating, we walked back into the front yard and waited for the party to be over.

Finally the front door opened and we heard voices. Daddy came out first, backing through the door, hunched over, his butt sticking out. Khakis sagging. He held his hairy arms out before him like he was coaxing a baby to walk or asking somebody to dance. Still slowly backing up. Then Mama made her appearance at the door. She looked blurry to me, out of focus. Strands of hair hung down over her eyes. Her feet slid out of her shoes. She reached out to Daddy, likes he was slipping away from her; then they connected, twining their fingers together. Mama swayed to one side, then to the other. We stood on the edge of the carport, watching. James made his hand into a gun, fired off a couple of shots at them, *pow, pow*ing under his breath, then ran over to the mimosa, jumped up high, grabbed a limb, and starting bouncing. The limb waved up and down like a giant fan. Pink flowers fell limp on the ground. I thought the limb would snap. I thought that was James's point, to snap something in half. Maisey and I didn't move. Troy said good-bye, hurried into the house and shut the door behind him.

By the time they dance-walked to the car, Mama was laughing so hard that we all started laughing, too. She was funny. We helped Daddy get her into the car, which wasn't easy; she kept springing out like one of those trick snakes stuffed into a peanut can. And she giggled like a little kid, pointing at Maisey and me, telling Daddy to *puhleeze get those girls away from me.* We finally crammed her into the car and Daddy hollered at James to come on and off we went.

The ride home was weird—Daddy was not-Daddy and Mama was not-Mama. She kicked her shoes off, swung her feet up onto the dashboard of the car, rolled the window down, leaned her head into the wind. Her hair blew back. Then she started bobbing, head and shoulders, singing "King of the Road" out of tune. "I jus' love Roger Miller," she said, turning to Daddy. "Dwayne, ya gotta buy me a stereo and some records, so I can dance."

"Okay, baby," he said. "Whatever you want."

By the time we crossed Victory Bridge, Mama had quieted down and by the time Daddy turned onto Satsuma Street, she'd fallen asleep and was limp as a rag doll. Her mouth hung open like a big gray zero. James helped Daddy carry her into the house and lay her on the bed.

For a minute the house was still and quiet, as if nobody was home. The clock ticked loud as a bomb. Daddy went outside and sat on the porch and smoked. Then James turned the TV on. *Hawaii 5-O*. He glanced at me and Maisey sitting on the couch, and went into the Jack Lord stance, holding an imaginary gun on us, using both hands. "Bookem Dano," he said, and sat down. Maisey and I didn't even move. Just about the moment when it felt like nothing else would happen, we heard the window in Mama's room scrape open. We walked back to see what she was doing. She was gone, the room empty. Like Jesus, risen from the dead. James walked over to the open window. The screen was popped out. He stuck his head outside and pointed downward with a smirk on his face. Mama had crawled out of the window and was squatting on the ground beneath the azaleas.

She wasn't laughing anymore; she'd changed from not-Mama to not-not-Mama. A dark mood had settled over her; I could see it in her eyes. They were black as marbles. Maisey was the first to try to get her back into the house. The sun hadn't set yet; anybody who looked at our house would be able to see her. Maisey leaned out of the window as if the house were a boat and Mama had fallen into the water. "Mama, come on. The neighbors will see you." James disappeared to his room and started blowing an out-of-tune "Summertime" on his trumpet, every now and then stopping to belt out the words *when the living's easy.*

I went outside and walked right past Daddy without saying a word to him; he wouldn't be any help; he'd helped her get this way. Mama sat hunched in a space beneath the dark green bushes, her arms circling her knees. I pushed the branches out of the way, squatted down next to her. A couple of the hot-pink flowers fell to the ground. "Mama, come back in the house," I said.

I touched her arm; her skin was dry and warm, but it didn't feel alive to me. Touching her was like touching an empty body. I tried again. "Mama, you've got to come in." I smelled the damp earth beneath us, that and flowers and the sour smell of alcohol. I touched her arm again, this time pulling on her; she was frozen; she wasn't going to budge. A dog barked in the distance.

She clawed at the dirt with her fingers. "I was the home-coming queen," she slurred. "Oh, Lily, I wanted that for you."

I thought she was joking and wanted her to laugh. I wanted to laugh. I didn't know what to say. I mean, she was sitting in the dirt beneath the bushes saying she'd been a queen and wanted me to be one, which was about as far from what I wanted as the moon. It wasn't the first time I'd heard it. She'd told me she'd been queen before, but she could never find the photographs to prove it. She'd taken me up to the high-school library one day, to see if they had the old annuals, and they did, but 1951 was missing. Instead, she showed me a picture of herself in the eleventh grade, then stood next to the row of yearbooks, rubbing her thumb along their spines. She'd finally given up dying her hair then, and it was just beginning to turn gray. It was hard for me to imagine her in high school.

Now, she slapped at the bush with her hand, then touched the top of her head. Her voice was loopy, like a song on a warped record. "I wore a diamond tiara," she said, and "Daddy and Mama lemme buy a blue satin dress. Jimmy Dolan was king; he's a state senator now. I could've married him instead of Dwayne, you know, and everything would've been different."

Even though the idea was impossible, it was appealing. Maybe if she'd gotten elected Miss Chattahoochee and married Jimmy Dolan, she wouldn't have gone crazy; maybe if she had ridden on a few floats she wouldn't be addicted to pills. If we'd had a different father we wouldn't be the same at all. Mama started crying.

She wouldn't budge when I whispered in her ear that I was sorry about Jimmy Dolan but that she needed to come into the house. Deep inside I wanted more than anything for her to find that photograph, to prove to me that she existed in 1951, that she wore diamonds in her hair and that there was a time when she smiled for a photograph, that she had been a queen, Mama a queen, the queen of homecoming.

"Let's leave her alone," I told Maisey, and she shook her head and started crying, too, backing away from the window, covering her face with her hands. The muffled sound of James's trumpet drifted out of the window, over Mama's head.

25

After I met the Lubjeks and fell in love with them, I tried to learn to lip-read. I stuffed cotton in my ears, turned the TV on, turned the sound off, and lay on the floor with a pillow wrapped around my head. Watched Walter Cronkite on the six-o'clock news but his mustache got in the way, that and Mama standing in front of me, wagging her jaws at me like a ventriloquist's doll: "What in the hell are you doing?" I knew then that Ronnie was lucky for lots of reasons. Not only could he sneak out of bed late at night and watch TV, he could call his mother stupid out loud as long as he looked the other way. And she didn't climb out of windows and sit in the bushes drunk. And he didn't have to paste a big smile on his face and act like nothing had happened.

Ronnie and I finally started hanging out together the summer after he moved in. After our parents went to work, Maisey and James and the rest of the neighbor kids walked down to the Teen Club and assaulted each other playing foosball and basketball all day. Ronnie and I had the whole neighborhood to ourselves. We rode our bikes all over town, even around the hospital grounds and I introduced him to Innertube and Peanut and told him how Peanut would answer "nine" no matter what you asked him. We ate tomato sandwiches and walked over to the playground and set fires, burning the dead grass with Ronnie's magnifying glass. We always came back to the damp, dark garage. I loved the way it smelled under there —like dirt and water and old wood. Sometimes when Mrs. Lubjek came home early, I could hear her footsteps above us, clunking from one room to the other like a ghost.

One morning Ronnie had to go uptown to buy some window screens for his mother, so I decided to go to the Teen Club for a couple of hours to shoot pool. It had just rained and muddy brown water gushed down the ditch that ran next to Satsuma Street. Wisps of steam drifted over the greasy black asphalt. As I walked down the hill, I imagined jumping in the ditch, floating to the bottom, but I knew I wouldn't float and this ditch wasn't as smooth as the one in front of our house; it was full of sticks and rocks. I stepped off the road to look in the ditch anyway, and there, drooped over the peppery-smelling grass, was a page torn from a magazine.

When I bent down to snap a blade of grass to chew, I saw that it wasn't just a picture from *Popular Mechanics* or *Good Housekeeping*, it was a picture of a woman, a naked woman. And she wasn't just standing there naked like somebody in the jungle. She was laying on a purple couch with her legs spread *wide open,* and she had a squeegy look on her face. And it was weird, but I thought of a used rubber I found in the woods behind the Teen Club. Thin and wilted as a snakeskin and yellowy-looking. It probably belonged to Lisa Atwater, a ninth-grader who bleached her hair and raccooned her eyes with mascara. Her mother let her go on dates with boys who drove vans. *Not a nice girl*, Mama said. I hooked the rubber onto the end of a stick and lifted it; I could see wet stuff in it and it was hard not to think of what it was and where it had been, and I felt strange but I couldn't help but look at it.

I couldn't help myself now, either. I looked and looked and looked at the naked woman. The little hairs on my neck stood up, and I looked and looked and looked and the gushing water disappeared and the black road disappeared and I was left standing there beneath the washed-out sky, a yinging sound in my head. I thought the noise was coming from the picture, but then I realized it was the cicadas going *yeeeeen, yeeeeeeen, yeeeeeeen*, and I folded the picture up and put in my back pocket and kept walking before somebody saw me.

When I got to the bottom of the hill where the trees grew over the road, I stood still for a second, listening for cars, then pulled the soggy picture from my pocket and crouched in the damp green shadow of a mimosa and looked at it again. Another chill went over me. I had never looked at a woman's body before, not even my own, and I couldn't imagine why someone would want to show her body this way.

I accidentally saw between my mother's legs once when I was about five years old; she got out of the bathtub, and bent over to let the water out. I looked at her behind and saw something I'd never seen before. She had a brownish-colored grasshopper between her legs. I didn't see the grasshopper's legs, but there it was, a grasshopper's body, and for a long time I wondered about this.

This lady didn't have a grasshopper; she had a pink butterfly, and I mean pink, like some kid had gotten at it with a Magic Marker. I stared at her until a car drove by out of nowhere and blew the page, fluttering, out of my hand. I didn't want to just leave it lying there for anybody to look at, so I picked it up and put it back in my pocket. I knew I would be in big trouble if Mama ever found it, but I couldn't throw it away. So instead of going to the Teen Club, I headed home, dug a hole in our backyard, and buried the picture there. To keep it safe. As if the photograph was a real woman.

A couple of hours later when I walked outside to empty the garbage, Ronnie called me over. He stood next to the garage, green snakes of kudzu climbing the wall next to him.

"Look," he said, backing into the garage, drawing me into the darkness. He dug a box of matches out of his pocket and struck one, holding it close to his face. His nose and eyebrows were lit orange from underneath. He looked like a creature from outer space. The smell of sulfur filled the garage. I saw the fuzz on Ronnie's upper lip and wondered if he'd ever grow a mustache. I wondered if he'd ever seen a picture of a naked woman. Boys were supposed to look at stuff like that.

"Big deal," I said, blowing the match out. A ribbon of blue smoke drifted through Ronnie's orange hair. "What are you going to do? Burn the house down?"

He smiled and reached for his shirt pocket. Pulled a rumpled hand-rolled cigarette out and waved it at me like a wand. He narrowed his eyes. "Wanna smoke a joint?"

I laughed. First the picture of the naked woman, now this.

I stood in the shadows next to the old tires and shovels. My belly tingled. Ronnie sat down on an old red backseat he'd pulled out of an abandoned car. He leaned back and struck a match, holding it out before him till the small orange flame steadied. He placed the joint in his mouth carefully, as if he were kissing it, then he sucked hard at the flame with his pretty lips. Holding the smoke in and coughing, he passed the joint to me. I sat down next to him on the car seat and took a long drag. The tip of the joint was moist from where his lips had touched it. I held the smoke in till I felt dizzy, and let it all out. I took another drag, sucking the smoke deep into my lungs, and handed the joint back to him. A seed exploded, sending sparks onto his pants. He brushed the ash away. We didn't talk. I wondered if I was feeling something. Was I stoned?

Ronnie took another drag and held it, his lips pressed tight together. Then he made a fish mouth, puffing blue smoke rings into the air where they changed shapes and floated through his hair. When he handed the joint back to me, I inhaled the smoke deeply, held it, then let it drift out of my nose, the way I'd seen actresses smoke. I knew I was feeling something now. Hazy. I thought of the naked woman again and got a funny feeling in the pit of my stomach. I'd get in big trouble if Mama ever found out that I'd buried that picture in our backyard, and that I'd spent the afternoon smoking reefer with a boy. But I didn't care. That was it. That was the feeling. I was tired of caring what she thought of me.

Ronnie and I started smoking reefer every day. He brought down some candles and incense and a transistor radio, and we sat on the old car seat in the dark garage, smoking and listening to WOOF, rock 'n' roll.

One day after we smoked, he leaned over and kissed me on the lips, then thrust his tongue into my mouth. It felt like a big thick worm and his mouth tasted of reefer and

Dentyne gum. We kissed for a long time, practically eating each other, leaning back on that car seat, listening to the Rolling Stones. We kissed without stopping, *I can't get no, satisfaction, and I tried, and I tried, and I tried, and I tried,* breathing through our noses, gripping each other, careful not to slip apart. I felt lke I was in a contest. I was floating. I was stoned. Images flitted through my head. The naked woman. I never told Ronnie about her, although I know he would've liked to have seen her. The naked woman dissolved and became Rae. The white-haired Rae. The one who acted like she was tuned in to a radio the day I met her. The one I kissed. I couldn't see her face the way it had been then; I could only see her the way she was now, raccoon-eyed, her dull, blond hair hanging down over her face. I must've just let my mouth fall open, because Ronnie broke away from me and said, "What's wrong? Did you fall asleep or something?"

"My mouth's sore," I said, rubbing my jaw. "That's the first time I've ever kissed anybody." As soon as the words came out of my mouth, I knew they weren't true.

"That's not what I heard," he said, leaning back.

"What are you talking about?" I asked.

"I don't know," he said. "Just something I heard."

"What?" I said. "Damn, don't play games."

"I heard," he said, rubbing his hands over his thighs, "that you used to play kissing games with that girl named Rae."

"Oh God, that is so stupid," I said, wondering if Rae had told people. "We practiced kissing each other one time. We were in the sixth grade. Jesus, Ronnie. That was almost three years ago. I was twelve years old. I pretended to be a boy. All the girls do that." I wondered if kissing between girls was supposed to be a secret. I knew other girls did it, but they never talked about it. "Don't boys do that?"

"Hell no," he said, screwing up his face. "That would be disgusting."

As I walked home, I felt paranoid. I wondered what else Rae had said about me. Every now and then when I thought about that photograph of the woman, I ended up thinking about Rae. A month or so after I buried the picture, I decided to look at it again. When I dug it up, I accidentally jabbed a hole into it with my spoon and the naked lady fell to pieces in my hand. That strange feeling fell away with her, and I felt guilty, but deep down I knew it wasn't because I looked but because I was sorry I'd let her get ruined.

26

I wanted to ask Ronnie what living with his mother was like but was too embarrassed to do it. I figured he knew what life at my house was like; he could probably hear us yelling at each other; he'd probably seen Mama crawling out of the windows, but if he did, he never said anything. A couple of times I'd almost got up the nerve to ask him about his mother when he called me on the phone; the black plastic receiver seemed safer than going direct.

Sometimes I wanted to call him at night and ask him, but Mama said girls can't call boys, and I said why not, I want to talk to him, and she shook her head and said in an even louder voice, "GIRLS CAN NOT CALL BOYS; IT JUST ISN'T DONE," and what I wanted to say was, *Why is it okay for you to do whatever you want without worrying about anybody else,* but instead I said "crap" and walked over to the window and stared at the apartment, its windows glowing blue and yellow. Mrs. Lubjek passed by the window and it hit me that she wouldn't have minded me calling at all. She was normal.

When I was over there, Mrs. Lubjek always smiled at me,

touched my chin, drew my face to hers when I talked. The more I got to know her, the harder it was to look into her pale green eyes. I felt as if I would fall right into them, the way I'd felt when I'd looked into Rae's eyes that time. There was something about Mrs. Lubjek. I couldn't figure it out.

Once, Ronnie and I sat on the black vinyl couch next to her, eating potato chips and watching *The Wild, Wild West* with the sound turned down. Ronnie had tuned his transistor radio to Rock 99. The Doobie Brothers sang "China Grove." Mrs. Lubjek smiled at me during commercials. When she wasn't looking, Ronnie would touch my thigh, his hand quick as a spider. With each touch, his hand crept higher and higher till he touched me right between my legs. The room felt electrified. We didn't say a word. I wondered what Mama would see if she came to the screen door and looked in. Three people staring straight ahead, music playing, a crumpled bag of chips on the couch between us. Or would she have seen that I was in love with these two people, that I loved them more than I loved her? She would've died.

That night after taking a bath, I stood in front of the foggy bathroom mirror, staring at myself through half-closed eyes, practicing those *True Romance* looks. Girls were supposed to part their lips and lean back and the guys would kiss them. Ronnie would probably crack up if I looked at him like that. *What the hell's wrong with your mouth?* Or *What's going on? Got something in your eye?*

"What's it like?" I asked Ronnie one day when we met to smoke a joint. By then we were making out every day, toking on Salems I stole from the Jr. Food store when we walked down to buy Icees. We'd turned into a regular Bonnie and Clyde. Ronnie would go to one side of the counter and ask for change for a quarter, and, quick as a snake, I'd slide a pack of Salems into my pocket, my face blank as an empty blackboard.

"What's what like?" he asked.

"What's it like living with your mother?" I'd wanted to ask that question for so long. Now that we were smoking reefer together, I felt like we had a bond, that *True Romance* kind of bond I'd felt when I first met him. We had a history together. We'd gone steady for over a year. We'd made out for hours in the garage beneath his house, his hands groping my body, rock 'n' roll blaring out of his radio.

"I don't know what it's like," he said. "I don't know anything else. What's it like living with four people who can hear your every move? I can't imagine living with people who can hear everything. My mother and I have a sort of secret language. She reads my mind sometimes. You know what they say about people who lose one of their senses, don't you? Blind people can really hear and smell; well, my mom can read minds. It's like this," he said. "Lay down and let me tell you something without using any words at all. Let me play doodlebug on your belly."

I lay back on the soft, powdery dirt, smoothing my shirt down, the dirt cool against the skin on my arms. "Don't tickle me," I said. "I hate to be tickled."

Ronnie smiled and kneeled over me in the dirt. "Since you can't lip-read," he said, "I'm going to teach you sign language." I closed my eyes and he traced a circle over my stomach with his finger, singing softly, "Doodlebug, doodlebug, come outta your house, your house is on fire." I was entranced by the feel of his hands on my body. I imagined I looked like one of those girls in the comics, my lips slightly parted, my arms open, my eyelashes fanned against my cheek, and I felt ridiculous.

With one finger, Ronnie spelled words on my legs and arms and drew pictures on my stomach. "Can you tell what I'm saying?" he asked.

I felt his finger drawing an "I" and a W and an A and an N and a T. I could guess the rest. "I want you," I said.

"You do, huh?" He reached out and pinched my nipple. I pushed his hand away. "I get to play doodlebug on you," I said. I wanted to be the one in control.

"You don't know sign language, do you?" he asked.

"I know more than you know," I said. He stuck his tongue out at me and lay down and closed his eyes, smiling. "Don't tickle me," he said in a girly voice. "I hate it."

He looked so small lying there in the half-dark, so thin. So pretty. He might've been a creature I'd trapped, a butterfly, a lizard, a lightning bug. I leaned over his face and looked at his eyelids. His eyes moved beneath them as if he were trying to see something. In the dim light, I could see tiny blue veins just under his skin. He had the longest eyelashes. I touched his shirt and began moving my hands over his chest; I rubbed his shoulders and his arms, let my hands slide down his sides to his hips. He was mine; I could do anything to him. I could hurt him. His eyelids fluttered. I felt the muscles in his legs harden as my hands moved over his rough jeans. Tickling his knees, I started back up his body and something got into me. I wound up writing the letters f, u, c, and k quickly around his belly button so he wouldn't be able to tell what I wrote. Then I stopped. His pants bulged out where his penis was. I got the same feeling I'd had when I found the picture of the naked woman, *don't look, don't look, don't look.* And then I looked. It was almost the same feeling I'd had right before Rae walked off with those boys: My mind had done a ping-pong number back and forth, back and forth, *rightwrongrightwrong.*

I wished I had a gun to point at Ronnie. "Take your clothes off, now," I'd say in a deep voice, pressing the metal gun to the side of his head. I wanted to put my hand over his mouth, fling his clothes off into the dirt, kick them into a corner. I wanted him to lie there while I looked at his naked body. I wanted to pinch his naked boy butt, jerk his hard, naked penis till blue bruises bloomed on his skin like roses. I kept hearing Mama's voice, *Girls, girls, girls. Girls are not supposed to; girls can't; girls shouldn't; girls don't, girls won't; girls never...* and I couldn't bring myself to do anything. Not even anything nice. I lifted my hands off his body and stood up. Ronnie opened his eyes and looked up at me. "What's wrong?" he asked.

I didn't know what to say to him. *I want to hurt you. I want to pin you to the wall because you're so fucking nice.* I only knew that I wanted to get out of that dark place as fast as I could. Away from that voice. Away from that feeling. As I stepped into the light outside, Ronnie called my name, *"Lilllllly."* I ran.

. . . . .

I swear Mama had radar. When she came home from work that afternoon, she found me sitting cross-legged on my bed, listening to the Moody Blues. After she'd gotten drunk at Bobby and Barbara's, Daddy had bought her a cheap little stereo, just like she'd asked him to. She listened to Cole Porter for a month or so, then quit, and James took a pencil and poked holes in the shiny silver cloth stretched over the speakers. Then Maisey and I dragged it into our room. "You're up to no good with that boy, aren't you?"

I twisted my head to look up at her, "What? Of course not, Mama. We're friends." I noticed a spider-shaped bloodstain on her uniform, right below her left breast.

She jabbed her finger in my face. "I know," she said evenly, "Boys only want one thing and they don't mind spending a little time to get it. Nice girls know that and they find other things to do, like taking up baton twirling or playing the piano. Look at Miss America. Baton twirling took her to the top. It pays to develop a talent instead of hanging around with some boy."

I stared at her. The White Rain had lost its hold on her hair; her curl was falling out. She looked tired, but she stood there nodding her head, as if she'd just said something profound. Was she serious? I thought of Miss America prancing around on a stage like a poodle walking on its hind legs. "I don't want to twirl a baton," I said.

"You're spending too much time with him," she said. I cranked the music up louder.

. . . . .

My feelings for Ronnie seeped into the house like smoke from a fire. Before long, it was Maisey's turn to burn the house down with a boy. She'd just turned fourteen and finally stopped hiding her smile with the back of her hand. She fell for a boy from Greensboro, and you would've thought it was perfect because Mama worked at the hospital with his mother. But it was the worst possible time, because that was the year Mama came up with her own boyfriend. It was as if she was jealous of us; she couldn't stand for us to have boyfriends. She started hanging out with Mr. Kaufmann, an eighty-year-old man with a head full of white hair and deeply tanned bow legs. She met him when he visited his looney wife on the ward where Mama worked. On her days off she'd go for long rides with him to towns with strange names, Yulee, Umatilla, Welaka.

Daddy couldn't stand it. When Mama was gone he'd stand over the stove cooking dinner for us, trying to hold it all in. Once it got to be too much and he slammed the lid down on a steaming pot of green beans and yelled at us, "Your mother's having an affair with that man."

It was the maddest we'd ever seen him. "Jesus, Daddy," Maisey said, "he's eighty years old."

But that didn't stop Daddy from being mad, and it sure didn't slow Mama down. She ignored Daddy and brought us back souvenirs, little jars of orange-blossom jelly, grass hula skirts, rubber alligators, hand-carved tomahawks, stuff we were way too old to want.

"He's showing me the real Florida," she said. "I've lived in Florida my whole life and I've never seen it." She told us stories about beekeepers and glass-bottomed boats and men who wrestled alligators. She said she'd never seen so many orange groves; one row of orange trees was fifteen miles long and so full of oranges you could taste the air.

Mr. Kaufmann drank whiskey and Mama started drinking with him. Except for popping pills, she'd stayed sober since the barbeque at the Carter's, but I guess after that experience, drinking bourbon with Mr. Kaufmann didn't seem so bad. At first she tried to hide it, like a kid, chewing gum and all. Then she just started coming home reeking of alcohol. I was home alone late one afternoon watching *The Brady Bunch* and she walked in, trying to act okay, but she wasn't; she jerked along like a puppet, her eyes unfocused, her face slack and pasty.

"Mama, are you okay?" I asked. Her head seemed disconnected from her body. "Maybe you oughta lay down." She didn't answer me but dropped the bag of oranges she held in her hand and lurched through the kitchen toward the bathroom, patting the walls to keep her balance. She bowed over the toilet, retching. I came in and stood beside her in the dim yellow light, the sour smell of bourbon and vomit filling the room, and I touched her back. Her spine curved downward.

When she finished, she sat on the floor, her eyes squeezed shut, then she slumped over, her pale face pressed onto the linoleum, her damp hair limp as rope. She was so still she might've been dead. I picked up her hand and held it in mine, looking at the knobby knuckles, the wormlike veins, the lines etched into her brown skin.

"Let go of me," she mumbled.

. . . . .

A couple of weeks later, Maisey's boyfriend drove over to see her one evening as a surprise. Mama had been out for a ride with Mr. Kaufmann that day and had come home late in the afternoon, very drunk. She'd taken a bath, draped herself in a thin white nightgown, then dumped so much baby powder on her chest, she looked like a piece of chicken about to be fried.

James had gone to a ball game with Daddy; they always got out of her way. We'd all more or less accepted that Mama was going to do what she was going to do and we'd just have to adjust. Basically, that meant acting like nothing was wrong. But the night Danny came to see Maisey, there wasn't any pretending. Mama walked out into the front yard wearing her nightgown and laid down in the damp grass curled on her side, her knees drawn up under her breasts, her hands folded under her head as if she was praying.

Danny rang the doorbell, looking over his shoulder at Mama lying in the yard, and Maisey peeped out the window, saw his truck, then ran to the bathroom to hide. I went to the door and said, "Danny, she's not going to come out."

"It don't matter to me," he said, nodding in Mama's direction. "That don't matter to me at all. I want to see Maisey; tell her to come on out here."

I left Danny on the front porch and went to the bathroom. Maisey had locked the door. "He wants you to come out," I said. "He says it doesn't matter; he doesn't care." I could hear Maisey sobbing behind the door. She screamed, "Tell him to go away."

"Come on, Maisey," I said, "it doesn't matter," and she screamed again, "Go away."

I walked back to the porch and stepped outside. I heard the train whistle in the distance, one, two, three times. The familiar rumble of boxcars moving down the tracks. Away. Danny sat on the steps.

Mama lay on her side in the grass. She still looked as if she was praying. It was dark out. "Mama has a thing about the yard," I said to Danny. "She likes to fall asleep beneath the stars." It was true. She did like the stars. One moonless night, Mama and I knelt in the backyard and looked up at the starry sky through James's telescope. She pointed out the Big Dipper, the Little Bear, the North Star, told me that some stars we looked at weren't even there anymore; they'd burnt out a hundred years ago. Later I would lay in the front yard alone, gazing up at a black sky sprinkled with the ghost-white stars of the Milky Way, wondering which ones were really there and which ones had burnt out.

"Let me go talk to Maisey," Danny said. He went into the house. I stayed outside and looked up at the sky. A thousand bright dots were scattered across the inky blackness. I couldn't believe the stars above me were the same stars Mama and I had looked at. So much had changed. In a few minutes Danny came back out. "She won't talk to me," he said, stuffing his big hands into his pockets. "I reckon I'll go on home."

"Okay," I said, and "Hey, next time call first." But that didn't matter because Maisey never would go out with Danny again.

27

The first time I saw Cat Reeves I thought she was a boy. She rode by the school right after the last-period bell, really strutting by in her jacked-up VW bug with those gangster whitewalls, the engine purring like a tiger, one of those naked metal ladies flying off the hood. Cat wore a big fluffy Afro and dark glasses, like she was one of the Jackson 5 or something. She carried herself like one of them, too, cruising by the school, looking at all the kids, really letting them look at her, and I looked and so did my friend Betty. All the eleventh-grade girls were interested in black boys right then. I had a poster of Michael Jackson on my wall at home. Even Mama thought he was cute.

When Cat rounded the corner at the end of the street, I turned to Betty. "That's a girl?" I asked.

"Yep. She almost got arrested one time for going in the ladies' room at a Sneads football game. Some old redneck woman thought she was a boy," Betty said, "Probably because she didn't have a beehive hairdo and nine-inch nails. Anyway, somebody ran and got the cops and they went right in and dragged Cat out. She was screaming the whole way, 'I'm a woman, you stupid motherfuckers.' Well, she probably didn't call them motherfuckers, but you know that's what she was thinking. Anyway, she ended up ripping her shirt off and showing her titties and they apologized."

I fell in love with Cat right then and there. A woman as strong as a man. A woman who would rip her shirt off. A woman who broke all the rules and didn't care. I started seeing Cat everywhere after I noticed her that first time; she coasted past me and Ronnie as we walked home hand in hand from school; she appeared out at the lake when Maisey and Betty and I went swimming. Once she walked out on the dock with her friend, a guy with gold teeth she called Mr. Dog. She wore low-slung blue jeans, and when she bent over to sit down, I could see the white rim of her underwear. I couldn't believe it—she wore B.V.D.'s "Why on earth are you wearing boys' underwear?" I asked, and she smiled and said, "Lasts longer." I was fascinated. I'd never met anyone who cared so little for what other people thought.

Cat's skin smelled like pine and she had muscles as big and hard as a man's from working at the sawmill. She pushed up her shirtsleeves and flexed her biceps for me and Betty, grinning slyly. Then she raised her shirt and let us look at the hard ripples on her brown belly while she swiveled her hips better than Elvis, bobbing her head up and down to the music blaring out of Betty's radio.

She told us where she lived, drew us a map, and whenever we could get away, we drove down the orange dirt road to her house and sat on her porch and drank tall glasses of ice water. Ronnie liked her, too. He drove me over to see her, and we held hands and smoked cigarettes and laughed at Cat's jokes.

Sue Baxter, who sat next to me in homeroom, told me that Cat was queer.

"No she is not," I said.

"She likes girls," Sue said.

"Everybody likes girls," I said, and Sue said, "No. She likes them a lot; you better stop hanging around with her or people'll think you're queer. Ronnie will, too."

"She's not a queer," I said. I liked her too much. Nothing could stop me from going to see her. Not even the threat of losing Ronnie. She was more exciting than any boy.

Sue tapped her fingers on her desk and looked at me as if my taking up for Cat meant I was queer, too. I didn't say a word.

A few days later at home, our washing machine broke down and Daddy didn't have enough money to get it fixed, so we had to lug our laundry up to the Laundromat at least once a week. But that ended up being a ticket out—whoever did the laundry got to take the car, and taking the car meant staying in motion for a little while.

I volunteered to go to the Laundromat every week. I got to where I knew the cycles of every washing machine in the place. I moved like lightning, shoved the clothes in a machine, dumped the detergent in, and hauled ass over to Sneads, to Cat's house. I couldn't have explained my desire to see her, and I felt guilty because I didn't even think of Ronnie. As I drove over Victory Bridge and down the red dirt roads to her house, I kept telling myself it didn't matter because she was a girl and I was a girl and we were just friends.

Once when I went over, we drank a couple of beers and she whispered in my ear, "Let me kiss you," and her face was so soft and so close, but I said "no," and she leaned even closer and said, "Let me kiss you," and I shook my head no. This was not the game Rae and I had played. Cat wasn't pretending to be someone else and she wasn't asking me to pretend to be someone else. She whispered the words again, her breath warm against my ear and I closed my eyes and turned to her and she kissed me, just like that, she touched her lips to mine. That kiss was so sweet and soft, so unlike any kiss I'd experienced before—even Rae's—that I'd drive over to Sneads and down all those dirt roads to her house just to kiss her once and drive home again.

I thought about those kisses all the time. When Ronnie pulled me into the garage and pushed me down on the old red car seat and kissed me, I felt like squirming away from him. Compared to Cat's soft lips, his whiskery mouth felt rough. But I felt guilty for kissing Cat behind his back, and I lay back in the dark and let him kiss me as much as he wanted to. I think he could tell the difference, though, that I was letting him kiss me instead of kissing him back. He started watching me when we went over to Cat's to drink beer, like he was waiting for me to slip up, to do something he could catch me at. One day he said he didn't want to go over to Cat's anymore—he'd heard she was queer and maybe she was. "Whaddaya think, Lily?" he asked. "Has she ever tried any funny stuff with you?"

I said no.

I knew I was about to get caught, though. Ronnie was easy to lie to, but I knew it was just a matter of time before Mama found out about Cat. She could read minds. She would tell Daddy what we were thinking, planning, or plotting, and most amazingly of all, she could predict the future, like the time she told Maisey she was going to have a boring life all because she wouldn't drink the eggnog she made, all because she spiked it with a little bourbon, and she was right. Maisey was scared of everything.

When Mama got really drunk, sometimes, she'd just come out and tell us what we thought or felt. *Y'all don't love me. Y'all wish I was dead. Y'all can't wait to leave me.* And we tried to convince her that what she said wasn't true, but sometimes it was hard, because she was right.

Sunday afternoon, me and Daddy and James were not watching golf on television. We were dozing. The announcer spoke in a hushed voice, almost a whisper; "We are at the ninth hole," as if he didn't really want anyone to hear him and it was such a sleepy day. Later *Godzilla* would come on and I'd fall asleep to the tinny soundtrack. But we never made it to *Godzilla*. Mama arrived home from work with a pint of Jack Daniel's hidden in her purse, and I guess the sight of all of us lying around the house, the curtains pulled, the dishes undone, the Sunday paper strewn everywhere, drove her to it; something drove her to it.

She changed clothes and came into the dining room gripping the bottle like a gun and held it up to her mouth, pouring. *Look at me, look at me,* and we did, but we were moving in slow motion. We didn't want Mama to drink because it was really clear that when she drank she became someone else; her eyes blackened, and I mean off one drink. All those years of Darvon; it was like pouring ink into water.

She was done before we could react, done, and out the door, already wobbling a bit, but intent, intent on leaving the house in broad daylight. This was a first; it was like she had gotten it all backward—she usually got drunk out and came in, but that day she was getting drunk in and going out. The front door slammed and Daddy sat up and looked at me and said, "We got to go get her."

I didn't want to go get her; I didn't want to go near her right then, but she was out there and we had to pull her back in.

Daddy and I walked outside. Mama was gone, nowhere to be seen. We piled into the Fairlane and headed uptown. Heat rose off the pavement in dizzy waves. We spotted her on Main street; she'd already made it to the Baptist church, swinging her arms like a monkey, leaning forward like she was walking into a strong wind.

We cruised up beside her, and I rolled the window down and said, "Mama, come on, let's go home," and she wouldn't look at me—she would've lost her balance if she looked at me—but I said it again. "Mama, come home, it's too hot to walk," and she said, "Y'all don't love me, and I'm leaving."

I looked at Daddy and he nodded ahead toward the next block. We could cut her off and get her into the car. He pulled around the corner and Mama kept walking; she just lurched around us.

Daddy coasted the car onto the side of the road and put it in park. He left the engine running and got out walking behind her. A giant black crow flew over him and landed on the top of a Dogwood, cawing loudly.

"Katherine, come on. Stop this." He talked to the back of her head. She kept walking. Every now and then she bumped into one of the azaleas that were planted next to the sidewalk, then jerked herself straight again. Daddy came back to the car and we started following her again.

I felt like we were in a big boat, floating up the street. We should've had a net; that would've done the job. A couple of cars passed us. Heads turned. We were going so slow, I could hear the electric whine of crickets. Hot air washed into the car. Mama wasn't slowing down at all, though. I think Daddy and I both wanted to stop her before she got uptown. Nobody was really out, just people doing their Sunday drives, but who wanted to be seen dragging their mama into a car?

"I'm going to get her on the next block," Daddy said, and he meant it. We went on ahead of Mama and turned right onto the next street. He parked on the grass in front of Mr. Creekmore's house, old Mr. Creekmore who was born with two club feet. Mr. Creekmore waved at us from his porch. A mangy-looking red rooster darted around the yard. Daddy smiled and waved back at Mr. Creekmore, told me through gritted teeth to open the back door. We were going to shove Mama into the car. He went toward her and grabbed her arm. Wrinkles of brown skin gathered at her wrist. She jerked around and screamed, "Goddammit, let me go," but he didn't and she dug her heels in like a little kid and he pulled her along screaming, "Nooooooo," her mouth wide open, and he kept pulling, his lips tight, his face so serious. Mr. Creekmore rose to his stubby feet, gripped the weathered corner post and watched. The rooster stopped pecking at the dirt and cocked his head in our direction.

Somehow Daddy got Mama into the backseat and pushed me in beside her and said, "Hold her," and jumped into the driver's seat and off we went. Daddy waved good-bye to Mr. Creekmore and his rooster.

Mama lurched toward the door handle, but I pulled her back. She was serious, she wanted out, and I was going to have to really get a grip on her, so I got behind her somehow and wrapped my arms around her body. Her rib cage surprised me. How hollow it felt. Her skin smelled of baby powder and bourbon. She kicked at the back of Daddy's seat with her white hospital shoes, screaming, "Let me go, let me go, let me go," and I held her tighter and she screamed even louder, "Let me go, you goddamn queer, you goddamn queer," and it was strange, hearing my own mama call me a name I hadn't thought of calling myself. I wanted to push her off of me, but I couldn't. Instead, I held her tighter, so tight I thought her ribs would break, and Daddy drove us home, Mama screaming the whole way, "I don't know how I ended up with a queer for a daughter; I don't know how I ended up with a goddamn queer."

When we pulled into our driveway, Daddy jumped out of the car and reached around to open my door. Mama lunged out of the car and fell over in the grass. One of her shoes came off. I stepped over to help her get up, and she swung her fist wildly at me, shouting, "Get her away from me, Dwayne. I don't want her near me."

There wasn't much I could say. I stepped back. Daddy didn't even look at me, like he couldn't bear to acknowledge the words. He worked at getting Mama on her feet. When she stood up, she glared at me. "The black women I work with said they wouldn't even spit on that filthy queer if she was on fire. I oughta tell your boyfriend what kind of trash you're running around with; he deserves better."

Daddy pulled her away from me and led her into the house. I walked behind them. James was still sitting on the couch not watching golf where we left him earlier. He didn't even look up from the television when Daddy marched Mama past him into her bedroom, not even when she looked over at him, and said, "Your sister's a queer." He nodded his head and took a deep breath.

Daddy didn't say anything about Mama calling me queer, either, but I didn't expect him to. He just filed that information wherever he filed stuff like the fact that Mama was crazy or that his own daddy had committed suicide. He was worse than lake water about swallowing things up, then going all smooth like nothing had ever happened.

28

Mama never said another word about Cat, about calling me queer. She never apologized, never looked at me funny when I went out with Ronnie. It was as if she forgot it happened, and maybe she had. A lot of times after she got drunk I could tell she couldn't remember things. But the words were still there, one more thing we'd never talk about, one more thing floating in the space between us.

She called me into the bathroom one evening a few weeks later. She was taking a bath in milky-blue water and I stood there, not looking at her but looking out the window. The room was filled with damp heat and golden light, the sloshy wet sound of water. Through the screen, I could see the sidewalk down the hill across the street; thick green wisteria vines heavy with purple flowers sagged beneath the trees.

"I saw the world's largest alligator the other day," she said, soaping her shoulder with a rag. "At Gatorland, down in Kissimmee. He jumped clear out of the water to get hold of a dead chicken some crazy lady dangled at him. Can you imagine having a job like that?" She splashed water onto her shoulders.

"You mean the gator or the woman?" I asked, thinking the gator got the worst end of the deal.

"I hadn't thought of it like that," she said, pulling the stopper out of the tub. The water began to glug down the drain.

It was getting dark. James and Daddy's voices echoed by the open window every now and then. They were playing catch; they'd play until it was completely dark, because James wanted to make the varsity baseball team. I knew how it was, how you could still see the ball when night was falling; how you couldn't really see it, but you knew it was there. Like my feelings for Cat and everything they meant. The thwack of the ball in their leather gloves sounded in the distance.

Mama got out of the tub and dried herself with a towel, patting her arms, her legs, her belly. Water gurgled down the drain. I glanced at her body; she was tan from head to toe. Even her breasts were tanned dark brown, and I tried to imagine the places she'd gone with Mr. Kaufmann, tried to picture my mother lying naked on a beach. She could do that, I thought; she could lie naked on a sand dune. She noticed me looking at her and held out her arm. "Carly says I'm going to be darker than her if I don't stop," she said, smiling. Carly was one of the black women Mama worked with, one of the women who said she wouldn't spit on Cat even if she were on fire.

"Well, you are pretty dark," I said, thinking how weird it was that white people like my mother would sweat their asses off in the sun to get as dark as black people. How dark skin meant different things on different people. It was weird to try to be something you weren't.

Mama wrapped the towel around her body; her skin was

still moist, her gray hair wet and curled around the ends. She propped one leg at a time on the edge of the tub and rubbed Jergens lotion onto her skin. Then she released the towel, let it drop to the floor, and rubbed lotion onto her arms, her belly, her breasts.

Reaching up to the shelf above the toilet, she took hold of the white plastic box of Johnson & Johnson baby powder, turned the top so it opened like a salt shaker, and dumped a pile of white powder into her hand. It was a big pile, a tiny pyramid. She didn't dust her body with it, though, but raised her hand to her mouth and ate it, licking her palm, her lips coated with white dust. That done, she shook a little powder on her chest and back, then got dressed.

I don't remember the first time I saw Mama eat baby powder; it was just something she always did, as if it were ordinary. Something strange, like climbing out of windows and sitting in the bushes. People could make the weirdest things seem ordinary: jumping alligators. Speaking in tongues. Getting a tan. Like Rae had said that day at the cabin: "It stinks but we'll get used to it, then we won't even notice the smell."

I wanted to know why Mama ate baby powder, too, so I tasted it myself. I poured some into my hand, touched my tongue to it. Mama pulled her pajamas on and smiled at me. "Tastes funny, doesn't it?"

The powder felt like chalk in my mouth, tasted faintly of perfume. Not ordinary, but something I could get used to, like the way it left the palms of my hands feeling like silk, soft and slippery. Like being queer.

29

When Mrs. Vanatter died, you would've thought she was part of the family the way Mama acted, crying and carrying on. It was as if her best friend had died, and in a way I guess she had. Mama never talked about anyone as much as she'd talked about Mrs. Vanatter. She was the sister Mama'd never had. Almost everyday, Mama told me something Mrs. Vanatter had done or said. Mrs. Vanatter had a purse made out of a dried up Armadillo; Mrs. Vanatter smoked rabbit tobacco; Mrs. Vanatter went to Niagara Falls on her honeymoon.

Who cares? I wanted to say whenever she tried to tell me something else about the woman. She was crazy. Her own family never even came to see her, and no one claimed her body when she died. That meant she was doomed to stay in Chattahoochee, buried like a dog's bone.

There was a secret graveyard for patients, just outside of town. Mama found out where it was and took me with her when she went to Nichol's Flower Shop to buy some lilies to put on Mrs. Vanatter's grave.

At the entrance of the graveyard, there was a gate and a

gravel road that was more ditch than road, and at the end of this gravel road, there was a field. If you just stood on the road and looked, all you could see were the crepe myrtles and palm trees lining the road and grass. The wind blew hard, rattling the palm fronds.

There weren't any headstones. At first Mama thought we'd come to the wrong place, then she noticed the sign on the corner of the field. It read *Section 1: 0–150*, and up the field were other signs reading *Section 2: 151–300, Section 3, Section 4, and Section 5*, all with numbers that went higher and higher.

Then we walked out into the field and saw them. Lying in the grass at the foot of each grave were concrete markers with numbers engraved on them. Mrs. Vanatter was easy to find because her grave was still mounded, orange with clay. She was number 2356. That kind of gave me a pang. I mean, I was tired of hearing about her, but to see her end up as a number gave me an empty feeling. Next to her spot was a metal frame the shape and size of a grave, already in place for the grave digger's next job.

"Oh," Mama said. "Oh, oh, oh. Number 2356." She waved her hand at the row of stones. "And there's 2355, and 2354, and 2353, and 2352. I wonder what number they'd give me if I stuck around. To get a number when you die is an interesting idea, isn't it, Lily? I wouldn't mind having one myself. Do you think they do it to save people the embarrassment of being crazy, or of having a crazy person in the family? They used to lock people in attics, you know."

I shrugged my shoulders. "It doesn't look like anybody ever comes here."

Mama dropped the flowers onto the orange clay, then

stepped into the metal frame next to Mrs. Vanatter's grave and lay on her back in the grass, her hands folded over her stomach. "Number 2357, come on down," she shouted. "I always wondered how they got the hole just right." She sat up and raked her fingers through the grass. "One size fits all, I guess. That's comforting. No matter who you are or what you did, in the end, one size fits all."

. . . . .

For a while after Mrs. Vanatter died, Mama's favorite song was Bobbie Gentry's "Ode to Billie Joe," about a man who jumped off the Tallahatchie Bridge. I think she felt bad that Mrs. Vanatter never left the hospital, and the song was Mama's wish for her. Jumping off a bridge into a slow-moving river was a way of fighting back, even if it meant killing yourself. Maybe this was why when Daddy let Maisey drive us over Victory Bridge Mama stopped telling us to look for turtles sunning on logs in the muddy water below and started talking about suicides instead. I looked through the dusty window at the cypress trees and willows growing at the edge of the river and thought of Cat instead, how I had to cross water to get to her house. That had to mean something.

Mama said people jumped off bridges all the time. "I read that thirty people jump off the Golden Gate Bridge in San Francisco every year," she said. "It's the most popular bridge to jump off. And then you have the Brooklyn Bridge and the Empire State Building. People like falling from famous places."

I wondered where she read this, if she looked it up or

something. She was on a suicide roll.

"I knew a patient," Mama said, "who just couldn't take living in the hospital anymore, so one night she tiptoed right out the door, right through town, past the Bait Shop. Wilder Watson said he saw her, said she was wearing a nightgown and a pair of yellow bedroom slippers. Said she looked fine. Well, she wasn't. She walked all the way down here and she climbed up on the railing and jumped. They found her body two days later tangled in a willow tree down near Torreya. She was barefoot; I bet those yellow slippers are floating in the Gulf of Mexico by now."

The way she told the story you would've thought the woman did something brave, like getting shot out of a cannon. I wondered why I hadn't heard the story before, wondered if Mama was making it up to make herself feel better about Mrs. Vanatter.

"Hitting the water hard is what kills them," Mama said, "or maybe they land on rocks or maybe they die of fear as they are falling." While Mama talked, I closed my eyes. Tried to imagine dying of fear. Did your heart just stop? Pictures of people jumping through the air took the place of alligators and turtles bobbing in the water below. My head filled with images of people falling through space. Of Cat, floating just out of my reach, of Ronnie, trying to pull me down with him, of Mama, always falling, falling, falling, never hitting the water.

30

Ronnie and I walked up to the hospital to watch a movie with the patients. We sat in the back row with two or three other couples. Our being in the auditorium was a secret; not many kids knew about the movies; they were for the patients, but we came along to watch. John Wayne, Jerry Lewis—we didn't care what was playing; the object was to sit in the dark. There was no concession stand; we didn't drink Cokes or eat popcorn or Jujubes or Junior Mints or Milk Duds. There weren't any red-velvet curtains dripping in curvy folds against the walls. It was just us, thirty or forty patients, and a couple of orderlies.

Waiting for the movie to begin, we leaned back in wooden auditorium chairs and looked toward the screen over a scattering of gray and bald heads. Behind us, an orderly who looked like Elvis Presley—slicked-back hair, rolled-up sleeves, and turned-up collar—set the rickety metal film projector on a table. A shrunken man with a curved back walked down the aisle next to me, clutching his bathrobe with a crabbed hand. I saw Peanut down near the front of the auditorium.

The boys laughed and talked and finally Elvis opened the metal film tin with a loud pop. I turned to look at him. He flexed his right bicep and gave me a quick wink as he snapped the reel into place. Then he fed the slick brown film into the projector with his fingertips. Someone flipped the light switch. The room went completely dark. When the film flickered onto the screen, scratched-up numbers scrolled by, crackling and snapping: 5-4-3-2-1. We got quiet. A few of the patients turned around to look at the projector. One man wagged his hand in the beam of light. That set off a whole string of hands bobbing in midair. "Look at those stupid retards," Ronnie said. I looked at the white hands, whiter from being in the bright light. Some of the hands bristled with gray hair. A voice from somewhere near the front of the auditorium said, "Get your goddamn hands down."

A few rows in front of us, another man kneeled backward in his chair, facing the light, staring the projector down, his possum-shaped face and eyes almost completely washed out by the bright light. The orderly behind us yelled at him, "Gunderson, get your head down. You'll go blind." The man next to Gunderson pulled him out of the light, just as the words *Red River* darkened the screen and tinny-sounding piano music filled the auditorium.

This auditorium had taken the place of the damp garage where Ronnie and I sat in soft dirt, touched each other, and smoked joints in secret. I came to this dark room to play the game I was supposed to play in the world, to sit in a row of boys and girls, to let Ronnie kiss me, fondle me, to whisper no and hope he knew I meant yes. He was all lips and tongue and hands. All hot breath and damp skin. Licking and loud, juicy smacks. Fingers pinching elastic. I was something to get at. He bit my neck, squeezed my breasts. There and not there, I floated to the ceiling and looked down, watched my body move in the dark with this boy.

Ronnie had recently started shaving, and the bristle on his upper lip hurt my mouth, felt like wet sandpaper. He wasn't as sweet as he used to be. I wasn't either. Once the movie started, he stabbed his hot tongue into my mouth and, bored, I opened my eyes and watched specks of dust whirl like confetti in the shaft of light beaming from the projector to the screen. As the projector whirred and clicked, I watched cowboys and their horses gallop across the screen behind Ronnie's twisting head, clouds of dirt rising in the air. Out of the corner of my eye, I noticed Elvis, the orderly, sitting across the aisle watching us instead of the movie. I didn't care.

Ronnie moved his tongue in my mouth, and my mind drifted. I thought of what Mama said about light: *Wave or particle? How'd they think to measure the speed of light? The speed of light?*

Suddenly John Wayne shouted, "Take 'em to Missouri, Matt!" and I imagined the cowboys hitting the screen at 186,000 miles per second. "Yee Haw!" Then I thought of Cat's kisses, soft and pillowy. I couldn't help myself. I knew I was supposed to like Ronnie kissing me, but I didn't. I liked him, but not those kisses because they didn't feel like kisses but like a mouth gnawing away at me, and I'd been gnawed at enough. Maybe I was a goddamn queer like Mama said, because I wanted Cat's kisses, camellia-soft.

Ronnie pulled away from me to catch his breath. A couple of patients walked up the aisle hunched together. I closed my eyes against the cowboys, waited for Ronnie to press himself against me again, waited for the credits to roll. The film ran out, the tail end of it whipping around and around with a *slap slap slap*, and the orderly got up and switched the projector off. Someone turned the lights on. Ronnie nuzzled his mouth against my ear as the patients shuffled by us, some wiping their eyes as if they'd been asleep, some laughing and talking to each other. One tall handsome man with a perfect mustache caught my eye and held it, and I felt him really seeing me—I felt him connect with something deep inside me, as if there weren't all that space between us. But there was. He was crazy. I wasn't. I turned away.

31

A few nights after Ronnie and watched the movie, I was supposed to be partying out at Lake Seminole with some kids from school, but instead I stole away from the bunch and thunked across Victory Bridge, fast, in my Daddy's yellow Fairlane to see Cat. Wind blasted through the car. Ever since Mama told me about that woman jumping off the bridge, I could never cross over it without seeing her perched on the concrete rail. Did she stand for a moment looking down the river before she jumped? Did the breeze ruffle her nightgown? Did she look down at her feet, and think, *Damn, I'm going to die wearing yellow bedroom slippers?* Every time I crossed the bridge, I thought of that woman falling through space, her body horizontal and still, her arms open, always falling toward the water.

When I got to Cat's orange dirt road, I turned and drove carefully past fences covered with blackberry vines. I passed the Blue Wave jook joint, turned again, then crept in moonlight up her road. I wondered what I'd say to her. *Hi, I just came to see you. Hi, thought I'd drop in.* Weird.

I'd seen her several times since she'd kissed me—once out

at the lake again. She walked up to the car with me, kicked the tires, called them Maypops. *Whatcha' doin' ridin' around on those maypops, girl? You ain't gonna make it home on those tires; they thin as balloons.* She smiled devilishly at me.

I saw her again at the Bait Shop. I was with Mama, so I had to act like I didn't see her. I walked past her car fast, looking at her out of the corner of my eye. When she saw me, she slouched back in her Bug like she was lounging in a La-Z-Boy, watched me walk in and then out of the door with a blue box of crickets in my hand, her dark brown eyes all over me, sticky as mayflies. She didn't say a word. When I sat down in the car, Mama was practically vibrating she was so mad. "That woman," she said, practically spitting the words out, "ought not to be allowed to walk down the street." I didn't say anything.

When I got to Cat's house, I pulled up in her yard. It didn't look like anyone was home. I got out, closed the door quietly, and walked right up to her porch. The front steps were gone, so I swung myself up and to the door. Knocking softly, I waited. Turned around, watched the lightning bugs blink green in the dark. The door opened. Behind it a dim yellow light. Cat stood there rubbing her eyes. She was wearing the kind of white sleeveless T-shirt my grandfather used to wear. "What the hell are you doing out here so late?" she asked.

"Came to see you," I said.

She stepped outside on the porch next to me. Looked at me. Rubbed her eyes some more. Stretched. Didn't say anything. I told her I was supposed to be at a party, couldn't stay long, and I asked her if she wanted a beer, but she didn't move, just watched me, the way she watched me that day she saw me and Mama down at the Bait Shop.

"Mmmm," she said. "Uh-huh. Just came to see me," she said. "Here I am; look at me."

Take a picture, lasts longer, said a voice in my head. I felt stupid then, ready to jump off the porch and get back to the boys; they'd probably gotten a fire going, were probably wondering where I was. Before I could make a move, Cat sat on the edge of the porch and motioned for me to sit next to her. She smiled. I sat down beside her, not too close but close enough that I could smell the sweet cologne she had on.

Cat put her arm around me, pulled me to her, whispered a warm *mmmmm* in my ear.

"I'm glad to see you," she said.

I felt too stupid to talk; I wished she'd put her other arm around me and pull me in tight. That's what I came for; she knew it and I knew it, but neither of us would ever say it. I kept thinking about the rules, what girls could and couldn't do, how boys were supposed to be the ones to call or to kiss or to hold your hand, and I knew she wasn't a boy but I felt like a girl around her, and I didn't know how that was supposed to work. I was a girl and she was a boy, but she wasn't, and that was why I liked her so much, the way she wasn't a boy. But I didn't know what to do with her.

Cat nuzzled her lips against my cheek, not kissing me, and I couldn't help it. I broke the rules. I turned to her and whispered, "Kiss me," and she did. She gently pushed me back on the wooden floor of the porch, kissing me deeply, her body rolling over mine, her breasts strange and soft. I couldn't help but wonder what would come next: What did two women do with each other after they kissed and kissed and kissed and kissed? We weren't pretending. Cat pressed her body hard against mine, like she was trying to push herself through me.

Like Ronnie but not like Ronnie at all. With him I left my body, but with her I was all there. Every molecule of me was alive. I wrapped my arms around her, felt the muscles tightening in her back. This was enough for now. I opened my eyes and looked up the moonwashed sky.

32

When I got back to the party at the lake, cars were circled around the orange light of the fire. People stood clumped together near the keg. The air smelled of smoke. Betty saw me getting out of the Fairlane and squealed, "Lilllly. Ronnie needed you and you weren't here."

She stumbled over to meet me. "Oh God, he was so drunk, Lily. They had to take him home. He was as sick as a dog. He should've never smoked all that reefer." She grabbed my arm and whispered loudly, "And you won't believe who's here."

I walked with her toward the crowd. Someone tossed a log onto the fire, sending up a cloud of sparks and ash.

"That Rae showed up. Drunk as a coot, too. All by herself."

"Where?" I asked. Then I saw her. Off to the side. Standing next to the dented silver keg holding a plastic cup full of beer. I wanted to run right over to her, to say, "Rae, how've you been?" but we'd ignored each other for so long, it was impossible. I wondered if she'd pretend she couldn't see me if I stood right in front her. She had before. She was good at making me invisible. I walked over to where she stood; she was talking to Kevin Keels.

I poured myself a beer and watched Rae as she laughed at something Kevin said. Firelight sparkled in her eyes. She saw me, then lifted her cup to her mouth so she wouldn't have to speak, half-smiled as she took a sip of beer. I noticed that her red fingernail polish was chipped, and for some reason that made me sad.

"What have you been up to?" I asked her.

"Oh, nothing," she said, looking into her cup as she swirled her beer around. "Just taking care of Mama." She cut her eyes at Kevin and they both started laughing. He moved closer to Rae.

I was surprised she mentioned her mother, but then Rae never had cared what anyone thought. Why should she now? Everyone knew she had a crazy mother; stories got told all the time. From what I heard, half the time it was Rae doing the telling. How her mama would leave the house in her nightgown, run out in the woods to see an oak tree with swirls in the bark that looked like Jesus; how she got the spirit at the Jitney Jungle, started speaking in tongues right there in middle of the frozen-food aisle.

"Must be hard," I said.

"Nothing's hard if you stay drunk enough," she said, and Kevin laughed loudly.

"You got that right," he said.

Everybody was drunk except me. Couples were lumped together under blankets by the fire, making out. I wondered why Rae wasn't with anyone.

I poured myself another beer. Watched as Rae walked away from the keg to go stand by the fire. Kevin watched Rae, too, looked her body up and down. In the orange glow of the fire, Rae looked like a shadow.

By two A.M. the party had pretty much fizzled out. Couples dragged themselves off their blankets, folded themselves into their cars, and went home. It was me and Rae and Kevin. Kevin was telling stories the way boys do, telling stories about himself, his voice loud and swaggering, but I wasn't listening. I'd heard that voice before—just a couple of days earlier at the movies—and there was nothing new there. I couldn't concentrate on him. Not with Rae standing next to me. I watched her like a movie I paid to see. I wasn't going to leave as long as she stood there.

She was very drunk. Kevin kept brushing his body against hers. He let his hand drift down to the small of her back. He cupped her ass. He curved his hips toward hers. Bumped her with his leg. Fingered a strand of her hair. Tried to make her laugh.

The fire was dying out and no one made a move to throw more wood on it. "Let's go," Kevin said, kicking a charred log back into the orange embers with the toe of his boot. A cloud of white ash swirled up in a puff of smoke, then settled on the ground. Kevin threw his arm around Rae, began moving her toward his truck. "See ya," he said to me over his shoulder. Rae's feet weren't working right, and she stumbled.

"Wait a minute," I said. "She's going with me. I'm taking her home." I watched my words turn into vapor in the cool night air. Rae looked down at the ground, her eyes smeared with a blur of mascara. "Lily, I don' wanna go wit you. I'm goin' with Kevin."

"C'mon Rae," I said. I tugged on her arm, pulled her away from Kevin. Her skin was warm. He tugged back.

I pulled Rae's arm even harder. I felt the hard bones beneath her soft skin. "Let go of her, Kevin. She's coming with me."

"The hell she is," he said, and he grabbed hold of her arm again.

We each had an arm. Rae was no help. Her head was bowed as if she were praying.

What I wanted do was to say to Kevin, "Let go of her, you stupid motherfucker, or I'm going to kick your ass," but I knew if I said that I *would* have to kick his ass and he was much bigger than me.

I jerked Rae's arm loose and led her over to my car, opened the door, and shoved her in, then ran around and climbed into the driver's seat. Kevin glared at me through the window. "You're jealous 'cause I don't wanna fuck you, aren't you?

"Yeah," I said. "I guess you could say that."

Then I floored the gas with Rae's door hanging open, and fishtailed across the damp grass away from the dying fire. In my rearview mirror, I watched Kevin punch the air as we drove away. A thin column of smoke rose behind him.

Rae, Rae, Rae. I looked over at her as I drove toward town. She slumped back in her seat next to the window; her eyes fixed on the floor, her hair blown crazy across her face. There was no way I could take her to my house—or her house, for that matter. Our mothers were both nuts, but they wouldn't like us being drunk one bit. I drove toward Rae's house, trying to think of what to do. We could spend the night in the car, but I didn't want to do that, either. As I bumped down the road past Rae's, I glanced over at her house. One window glowed with a yellow light. I wondered if Mrs. Miller sat up praying for Rae. I wondered if she worked herself into speaking in tongues at home. I looked over at Rae again; she'd fallen asleep. We'd have to go to our old shack.

I pulled into the grass where we'd danced naked in the leaves.

I had a couple of blankets in the car; I'd make Rae a bed inside on the floor and I'd sit up. I couldn't fall asleep. I had to have the car back early, before Mama or Daddy woke up and saw that it wasn't there. I left Rae in the car and walked up to the shack to see if it was still okay to hang out in. When I opened the door, the smell of rotten wood carried me back to that first day Rae had brought me here, when she had said, *We'll get used to that smell and we won't even notice it,* when she had put on her tap shoes and clacked across the floor, waving her arms in the air and laughing her big goofy laugh. She was a wonder to me. The way she claimed that house as ours. I wanted the confidence she had back then.

I laid the blankets out on the dusty floor and went back to the car to get her.

The air outside was cool and damp. Rae was heavy, hard to move, but I got her out of the car and pushed her up the steps into the house. Her hair smelled like wood smoke. When I lowered her onto the blankets, she rolled onto her side, drew her knees up, and curled into a ball. I sat down. Pale moonlight washed in through the broken window, casting a white glow on everything in the room. I looked around to see what was left from those days when Rae and I met here to play. Scattered across the floor were torn-up magazines and a couple of books. Shards of glass. Red rocks. Then I saw my old Tampa Nugget cigar box in the corner. I wondered if the bugs were still pinned inside it, and walked across the room the pick it up. It was coated with a fine gray dust. Slowly I lifted the lid, and there they were, the same beetles and butterflies, except for a few missing legs and a couple of faded and broken wings. *They had an easier time than we did,* I thought, *and they lost things, too.*

Rae stirred on the blankets and made a low moaning sound. She furrowed her eyebrows as if she were irritated. I stood over her, holding the cigar box. I had lost her. I remembered the day we kissed each other in that field, how I lingered over her face, looking at her white eyelashes, her smooth, white skin. Her skin had lost its translucence—I could no longer see the tiny blue veins crisscrossing that space just below her ear. I really wanted to kiss her that day, not just as a game, but to kiss her because I liked her so much. It hadn't been the same for her; it was just a game, the way our dancing naked or playing cowboys was a game. I wondered if she'd gone with those boys that day to show me just how much of a game it was for her.

If I could take my kiss back, I would. Maybe none of that stuff with those boys would've happened. But Rae would have to take things back, too, the way she whispered in my ear, *I've got something to show you,* the way she talked me into taking my clothes off and running out into the cold air. *Come on! Nobody's going to see you. Don't be a damn sissy.* I misunderstood her. Even though I thought we wanted the same thing, we didn't.

And I knew that now, watching her sleep. I looked out a streaky window at the sky as it grew a lighter and lighter gray behind the net of tree branches, then leaned back against the wall, thinking of kisses. Rae's, Ronnie's, Cat's. How Cat and I had kissed earlier tonight. How long ago that seemed. *Oh my God,* I thought, *I kissed a woman, put my tongue in her mouth.* As weird as it was, that kiss didn't hurt the way Ronnie and Rae's kisses did.

The sky changed colors from a washed-out gray to a lavender. Lavender gave way to streaks of delicate orange. Each color had a different effect on the room and on me. When the room was bathed in soft lavender light, I thought of waking Rae up to talk to her about what had happened between us—it seemed so fuzzy to me. Hadn't we been friends together? Didn't we have a house together? But when orange light poured into the room, illuminating the dust on the floor, casting shadows, talking to Rae didn't seem like a good idea. I remembered all the times she walked past me in the hall at school, not seeing me. Clearly, things weren't fuzzy to her. She wanted to let the past sink like a body into a lake, and who was I to make it any different? When the sun came up clear and yellow, I decided to leave, to let Rae sleep curled in watery light. I figured she could get herself home now.

33

Monty Hall chose a man in a chicken suit to play *Let's Make a Deal*, and I was dying. At least this was what I thought as I watched the chicken man flap his wings. I didn't get my period that month, and since I was still a virgin, it could only mean that there was something seriously wrong. Betty knew a girl whose period stopped and she had to have a major operation to keep her alive.

So I was lying in sunlight on the rug in the den watching Mama sweep, wondering how I was going to break the news that I was dying to her. She might've predicted who I was, or who I was going to be, but we'd never discussed bodies, except for those of patients who'd jumped off Victory Bridge. Mama taught Maisey and me how to bleach the rust stains off porcelain sinks, how to get the lint off rugs, how to defrost the refrigerator, but she had said nothing to us about blood, breasts, or hair. She swept. The light was golden and she stood at the center of it, surrounded by thousands of whirling dust motes. With each stroke of the broom, she stirred the dust and it swirled around her, up the sides of her body, over the top of her head. None was visible in the shadow she made. She was the dark, black center of the starry Milky Way.

That day she was cleaning the whole house—a spring cleaning, she said—but really she was just trying to get through the day. She hauled the mattresses outside and propped them up on chairs in the sun; she beat rugs and washed windows inside and out, hung the laundry on the line, scoured the oven, and scrubbed the toilets with her bare hands. That she was a woman who would rather put her hand in the toilet than talk to me about blood relieved me. I didn't really want to talk about it, either. Not with her.

After sweeping the den, Mama moved on to James's room, where she bent over the bed she'd just hauled back into the house, tucking the sheets in. I stood in the doorway. "I think something's wrong with me," I said. "I didn't get my period this month." I imagined Mama rushing over to me once I told her, throwing her arms around me, rubbing my forehead and whispering, "Oh, honey, you'll be okay."

But she didn't. She dropped to James's bed and sagged over, clutching her head in her hands. "Goddammit," she said, "you're pregnant," which was even stranger than the time she called me a queer. I thought she should make up her damn mind.

"What?" I said. "Pregnant?" I didn't think I heard her right. "I can't be pregnant; I've never had sex, Mama."

She looked up at the ceiling, moaning, "Jesus, what I have done to deserve this? Where did this girl come from?" She looked at me as if I were from outer space.

It was clear that my words were empty as air to her. Then she jerked her head at me. "You're just going to have to get a pregnancy test," she said. "I can't believe you've done this.

I told you you were spending too much time with that boy. Wait'll I tell your father."

I didn't want to be anywhere near the house when she told Daddy. I walked outside. It creeped me out to think of them discussing my body as if it had a life separate from the one I lived in it. It reminded me of the day I drowned, how Mama told a story so different from what actually happened. As I walked down the street, I pictured her and Daddy small in our backyard. Daddy scaling fish beneath the pecan tree, his skin and hair flecked with silvery fish scales. Mama lying in the grass, arms and legs splayed out like a kid making a snow angel. *Lily doesn't know it, Dwayne, but she has a baby growing in her belly, a tiny blue fish baby. It must've gotten inside her when she fell in the lake because she says the boy didn't put it there, but I know better, Dwayne, and we have to do something with her body to get the fish out. Daddy held a limp silver fish up by its tail and with one swipe cut its head off.*

. . . . .

The next day it rained and rained and rained. The air around us turned into water. Daddy drove me down the flooded highway to Tallahassee to get the pregnancy test. Over the sound of the windshield wipers whipping back and forth, he said he believed me; he knew I wasn't pregnant. I was so embarrassed to hear those words: "I know you aren't pregnant." It was like he'd been spying on me and Ronnie or something; he'd thought about whether I'd had sex or not. I couldn't even look at him. There was no way I was going to talk about sex with him. But I wanted to scream,

"If you believe me, then why are we driving to Tallahassee in a goddamn flood?"

The look on my face must've given my thought away, because he said, "Your mama would feel much better if you went ahead and got the pregnancy test, so why not just do it and make her happy?" The way he stared out the rain-glazed windshield, he reminded me of a stuffed deer with marbles for eyes. I knew he couldn't see anything in front of him except a blur of gray. I wanted to ask him why he didn't just go pee in the cup if he wanted to make Mama happy. I felt sorry for him right then, for being so stupid, stupid, stupid to think anything would make Mama happy. I'd been crawling to her side my whole life, saying I was sorry for things I never even did. The pregnancy test was just more of the same.

He parked the car on the street, and we ran through the rain into the doctor's office. We got soaked. Rain dripped from my clothes onto the floor. The nurse gave me a paper Dixie cup and pointed me toward the bathroom. I squatted over the toilet and held the cup close to my body. *It's strange,* I thought, *that piss would hold the answer to Mama's question.* I peed in the cup like the slut Mama thought I was, then carried the warm cup out to the nurse.

Everyone in the doctor's office thought I was a slut, too. Their eyes blared at me. *She's been doing it; she's a dirty little girl.* The nurse told me to sit down and wait for the results, and I wanted to tell her, *I know the results,* but I knew she wouldn't believe me. I sat down next to Daddy in an ice-white room and waited. He thumbed through a copy of *Field and Stream,* looking intently at photographs of dead animals. Nothing felt real. I started thinking, *What if I am pregnant? What if something weird happened when Ronnie touched me?*

In a few minutes the nurse came out of the back room and said, "Well, you're lucky this time. The test is negative." I wanted to cry, to tell her I didn't feel lucky.

Daddy didn't say a word on the ride home. The rain had stopped falling, but water puddled the road, ran fast through the ditches. When we got home I walked right past Mama and went straight to my room. She looked around me to Daddy, who shook his head no.

"No what?" she said.

"She's not pregnant."

As I slammed the door to my room, all I heard her say was, "She's lucky," and I wondered if everyone in the world was crazy except for me.

34

When I told Ronnie what had happened, he laughed. "Jesus, and I lost my reputation for nothing." We were sitting in the backseat of his mother's brand-new black Electra next to the dam where seagulls fluttered like paper in the wind above the muddy river. After not having a car for years, Mrs. Lubjek bought a huge boat of a car, the backseat as big as a bed. She said it made her feel safe.

Ronnie said the car made him horny. All that space. The musky smell of leather. Me and him. Almost a private room. *We can stretch out here.* He rubbed his crotch when he said this. I'd never touched him there on purpose. I wanted to that time in the garage, but I didn't. I wanted to see him naked then, too.

I guess the thought of me having a pregnancy test really turned him on—as if we really had done something, instead of just being accused of it. That evening he whispered softly in my ear, scratching his whiskers against my skin, "Baby, I know we can't go all the way, but there's something I need you to do for me. Baby, please." He said other girls did it; it was what girls did when they didn't want to lose their virginity or risk getting pregnant. I'd never have to worry about my mother again—plus, it would keep his balls from turning blue.

I didn't know what "it" he was talking about at first. I wasn't supposed to. Knowing what boys wanted and giving it to them meant you were a slut. I considered doing it, whatever it was. I considered that blue, those girls, and I looked at Ronnie's freckled face and imagined it turning blue also, imagined how his orange hair would look next to blue skin and wondered if his freckles would turn a darker blue or stay as they were?

We kissed, and he touched my breasts with one hand; with the other he stroked between my legs. "All you have to do is suck it," he said. He grinned. "Just like a lollipop."

I knew girls that'd done it—Betty had, and she said it gagged her. "I don't know about this," I said, sitting up straight, "don't know if I want to do this," but he insisted. Putting my mouth around his dick was a way out, he said, *This way, you keep your virginity; this is the way everyone does it.* There was so much talk about virginity, always the girls', never the boys, as if boys didn't have anything to lose.

I thought about it for a moment. *Didn't this mean I'd lose my virginity?* I didn't see how sucking a dick couldn't. *What was the difference between a mouth and a pussy? Wasn't that a riddle?* I tried to remember the answer. *No boy will marry you.*

Mama already thought I was a queer and a slut, so I didn't see the point of saving anything. I didn't know what I was, queer or slut, didn't know which one was worse. So I said, "Okay, I'll try it," and Ronnie sat up quickly and unzipped his pants. His penis sprung out, pale and hairless. I touched the tip with my fingers. It felt like silk, and I thought, *This won't be so bad,* and I bowed my head over his penis and I couldn't help it, it was like I was at the dinner table, about to try a new dish, so I sniffed him. I swear I couldn't help it and there was no smell, but it was too late. Ronnie noticed this sniffing and said, "What? Does it smell?" and I said, "No, but I don't want to do this. I can't do it."

"Jesus Christ," he said, leaning back. "Are you sure you're not queer?"

"Of course not," I said. "Godammit, Ronnie, I just had a fucking pregnancy test."

"I know, I know, I know, I know, I know." He ran his fingers through his hair, gave me a look as though he wasn't quite sure what I meant. "We might as well do it," he said. "I mean, your mother already thinks we did."

I didn't say anything. I noticed a small tear in the seam on the back of the passenger seat.

"C'mon," he said, his voice scratchy and low, "you gotta give me some relief. Here, give me your hand," and he clapped my hand onto his dick with his and started pulling. Then he let go of my hand and pushed me over and began kissing me again. He unzipped my pants and slid them down past my knees and rubbed my belly. Then he pushed his fingers up inside me and it stung, burned as though the skin was stretching. He dragged his fingers in and out of me and I held onto his penis, surprised at how hard it was, and how soft his skin was. I didn't care what happened. My mind filled with voices. *What was the difference between a finger and a dick? What was a virgin, anyway?* You sure couldn't tell one by looking at them. Betty said her boyfriend Charlie's come looked like the Crisco we smeared on our bodies instead of suntan lotion. She was a virgin.

I wanted Ronnie to do whatever he wanted to just like every other boy. *See, I'm not queer,* I wanted to say. *I'm not queer.* It didn't matter. What was I saving myself for? My mother could go fuck herself. I reached down and pushed Ronnie's hand away from my body. "No," I said. He groaned.

I pulled him on top of me. Hugged him close to my chest. Surprised, he lifted his head for a second. "I don't want to do that," I said. I rubbed my hand in circles on his back. *Just do what you want,* I thought. I kept rubbing his back. He shifted his body, placed himself between my legs, moved his hips up, then slid into me and it didn't even hurt; it wasn't really any different than his fingers, but it made me catch my breath. I guess I was supposed to feel as though I was losing something, but I didn't. I was pissed off, and it felt good to let him grind his body against mine, to prove I wasn't queer. Then his body went rigid and heavy and he fell onto me, moaning from deep in his throat.

. . . . .

When I got home that night, I headed straight for the bathroom. This I needed to check out. I took Mama's mirror down, flipped it to the magnifying side, and pulled my pants down. I sat on the edge of the bathtub and held the mirror between my legs. I looked at the soft folds of pink skin, wondered if it was possible to tell if a girl lost her virginity just by looking at her. I had no way of knowing whether my body looked different or not. That was the first time I ever really looked at it. *What does virginity look like, for Christ's sake?* I thought as I put the mirror back up on the counter. And I couldn't for the life of me understand what the big difference was between a penis and a finger. Why one caused you to lose your virginity and the other didn't. I thought of Cat and wondered if she'd ever done it with a boy. If she hadn't, did that mean she was a virgin? And if she never slept with a boy, would that mean she'd be a virgin for the rest of her life? Did she even care? Did I?

35

The next night I snuck out to be with Cat. As I walked down the sidewalk past a fragrant tangle of wisteria, I thought, *I'm getting to be a regular slut.* Then I said the words out loud, quietly, my voice low and deep. "You are a slut." But I didn't really feel like a slut. Sluts wore lots of greasy makeup, smeared their lips red, their eyelids blue, to attract boys. They arched their backs, flicked their hair. Were deliberate. I just let something happen. I didn't go looking for it, like a slut would.

But I was walking down the sidewalk to get into the car of a woman who kissed me. Who I kissed. I didn't think you could be a queer, either, if you just let things happen. It was all in the way you did things. I thought of how I had kissed Rae when I was twelve. We were supposed to pretend to be boys. When it was my turn, I pretended to pretend. Deep down I wanted to kiss her. I didn't think the kiss meant I was queer. It didn't mean anything to her.

I walked past a field where I used to ride my bicycle, pretending it was a horse. Mimosas arched over my head, their slender branches gently lifting in the breeze.

A voice chanted inside my head. *Boy/girl/boy/girl/boy/ girl/boy/girl. What?* I wanted to scream. *What? Skin is skin is skin is skin.* My grandmother had called all babies "her" or "she." *They're all girls at the beginning,* she said. I thought she was too lazy to remember their sex. *If a mother closes her eyes,* she said, *she can still pick her baby out of a crowd of babies using her sense of smell.*

Can she smell the difference between a girl and a boy? I asked.

If you close your eyes, can you tell the difference between a boy and a girl by touching their skin?

I worried about these things as I walked to the end of Satsuma Street to wait for Cat to drive up in her Bug.

I heard the *bluhbluhbluhbluhbluhbluh* of her engine from three blocks away. She zipped up next to me. The whole car vibrated. I climbed into the bubble of sound.

After being in Ronnie's Electra, Cat's Volkswagen seemed extra-small. Tight. Like the cockpit of an airplane. We buzzed uptown. Two patients and an orderly walked slowly across the darkening field toward the hospital. I imagined the patients arriving at the tall, white door of their ward, wondered if they felt like they were at home.

We rode out into the country. Cat kept looking over at me, not saying a word. I turned away, glanced out my window. Black sky. White stars. No. The sky wasn't black and the stars weren't white. Nothing was ever that clear.

I wondered if Cat could look at me and tell I'd lost my virginity. *Where did I lose it?* You were a virgin and then you weren't anymore. Mama thought she could tell.

Cat swerved the Bug onto a dirt road. "You're quiet."

I nodded. We were getting close to the lake. I could smell

the fishy water. I remembered how it tasted the day Mama let me drown. Green. When I told Cat about my drowning, I thought she would laugh at what a stupid white woman would do to her own daughter. She didn't. *White folks are mean as hell,* she'd said.

Mama and I never even talked about her letting me drown. She'd laughed it off when I mentioned it to her once. A lot of time had gone by, but I still hadn't seen any humor in my sinking to the bottom of that canal, green bubbles washing over me, Mama fish-white, her eyes, her hands guiding me down, down, down.

Cat pulled up next to the lake and stopped. Even though it was dark, the moon cast enough light that the sky looked like lace stretched behind the black branches of the trees. Spanish moss hung from the limbs of oaks like ghosts. We walked down to the edge of the lake and sat on a concrete picnic table. Cat said softly, "Don't wanna talk?"

I didn't want to talk. After all those words Ronnie threw at me—*This is how you remain a virgin; this is how you suck a dick; this is how you...*—I wanted to float soundless through the humid air. Cat kissed my ear, let her lips brush against my cheek. The air was noisy with the croaking of frogs, the chirruping of insects. A slow breeze blew silver ripples across the lake. Cat touched my hand with the tips of her fingers. Her skin was warm.

Once after I'd been with her, I touched the skin on my arm softly to see what it was she felt when she touched me. What was it?

Just then a car swung into the parking lot above us, crunching gravel. The lights shined into the trees next to where we sat. A door slammed. Leaves crackled as someone walked across the grass. I saw the silhouette of a person; the walk looked familiar. Loopy.

The voice came out of the dark. "Goddammit, I knew I would find you here."

She was drunk. Before I could say anything, she lunged out of the darkness at me, her face scrunched up in rage. She dragged me off the table into the grass. I tripped over a big rock but managed not to fall. She dug her fingers into my shoulders like claws. Cat rose to her feet. "Hey!"

"Get away from me, you queer," Mama said. She grabbed a handful of my hair, twisting it into a knot, then wrapped her other arm around my shoulders, making little grunting sounds with each motion. I felt her breath on my neck, smelled the sour odor of bourbon. She tightened her grip on my hair, began moving me across the grass. She stopped for a second, turned to face Cat. "You need to stay the hell away from my daughter."

I wanted to look at Cat. I knew she was standing in the dark, watching me. There wasn't anything she could do but watch. I let Mama march me to the car. I figured she was getting back at me for the time me and Daddy dragged her off that sidewalk into the car. I guess she thought the same thing we did: *If we can just get her into the car, everything will be okay.* We didn't know. She didn't, either. She drove me to the house without saying a word. I didn't care what she knew, or what she did to me. She couldn't get inside me to make me different.

When we got home I felt tired, like I'd been awake for a million years. Just then a train sounded its whistle; I could hear the low rumble of boxcars moving down the tracks. I wanted so badly to run down to River Junction, to fling myself onto the train, to roll away.

Instead, I walked into the house without waiting to see what Mama was going to do. I figured I'd just go to bed. The room was hazy with smoke. Daddy sat at the table next to an ashtray full of cigarette butts, and James and Maisey sat watching *Medical Center.* A siren blared out of the TV. The front door slammed. Daddy flicked an ash. James looked up at me. I wanted to be him—nothing ever happened to him.

Suddenly, the room exploded. Mama charged me from behind, struck me as hard as she could on the back of my head, drummed me to the floor with her fists. Then she bent over me and snatched a handful of my hair, jerking me off the floor with one hand. Pressing her body against my back, she stuck her face over my shoulder. We stood cheek to cheek. Her skin was dry and hot and she smelled of Jergens lotion and alcohol. She turned my body toward James and Maisey. When she spoke, her voice came out of her mouth low and guttural. "She's a goddamn queer. I won't have that in this house; I'll kill her first."

Maisey leapt off the couch, ran past us into our bedroom, and James and Daddy approached Mama slowly as if she were holding a gun.

"Katherine," Daddy said. He reached toward me with his thick fingers, a grim look on his face. Mama twisted my hair even harder. My neck ached; my scalp throbbed; I wondered if my head was covered with knots. "Katherine, you've got to stop this," he said.

"No, she's gotta stop," she said, and then screamed right into my ear, *"or I'm going to kill her."* Her breath was hot and sour and wet.

"James," Daddy said. "Grab her arm."

James lunged at Mama, clutching at her arm with both hands. When he pulled her away from me, I felt a clump of hair tearing away from my scalp. Daddy circled her, pushed her backward with his heavy body in an awkward dance. Her hands clawed the air behind him, strands of my hair clinging to her fingers. He hugged her tight and moved her toward their bedroom, her voice a ragged wailing, words spilling out of her mouth as though she were speaking in tongues.

James touched my shoulder with his hand. I cried.

. . . . .

A couple of days later, Mama came into my bedroom all business and concern. Like the *Brady Bunch* mom. I hadn't left the house since the night she attacked me. Maisey would hardly look at me. Daddy asked me how I felt once. The question seemed too big to answer, so I said "okay."

Mama stood in the door to the bedroom, told me she was sending me to a counselor. "To talk about your problem," she said. "You don't want to end up in a mental hospital, which is what's going to happen if you don't change your ways. I see it every day at work." She sighed. "I care about you, honey." I nodded, then reached up to my head and rubbed the quarter-sized spot where she'd torn my hair out.

She and Daddy both took me to the counselor. We drove to Quincy, and they walked me down the sidewalk to a brick storefront. Cars whooshed by. Across the street, a couple of boys walked along, bouncing a ball. Nothing felt real to me. I watched myself walking down the cracked gray sidewalk. A mockingbird flew over.

The waiting room was dark and musty. There wasn't even

a receptionist. Mama and Daddy went in to talk to the guy and I sat and flipped through a *Seventeen* magazine, reading the headlines: *My breasts won't grow; What's the coolest shirt for summer?* I tossed the magazine back onto the table, pulled the curtains back, and watched the traffic.

Then the door opened and Mama walked out, smoothing her dress down. Daddy followed her. They sent me in. A dying African violet sat on the windowsill in the counselor's office, its velvety leaves curled and black around the edges. The counselor's desk was stained with water rings. He motioned for me to sit down. I sat in a leather chair across from him and studied the brown curls of his beard. He tugged at his mustache. He was younger than either of my parents. He studied me. I waited for him to tell me I was disgusting. He didn't. "So," he said, leaning forward.

"Your violet's dying," I said.

We saw him for six weeks. I didn't tell a soul, not even Ronnie, and I couldn't tell Cat, because Mama wouldn't let me use the phone or go anywhere by myself except for school. Mama and Daddy would drive me over to Quincy and they'd go in and talk first, then they'd come out and give me these weak smiles and watch me go in. I told the counselor about my drowning, about Rae, about Ronnie and Cat. About Mama's drinking and pill popping and how Daddy just went along with everything. I told him how I'd had to have a pregnancy test before I'd even lost my virginity. During our last visit, he leaned back in his chair and put his feet on top of his desk. "I've talked to your mother and father and you. The best advice is advice I can't give you. I can't tell you to run away. But get out of there as soon as you can."

time I went somewhere. I could come and go as I pleased. James was busy trying to become a baseball star, and Maisey busied herself with school, trying to be the perfect girl. Daddy never paid attention; he paid even less now.

The third day Mama was gone, I walked across the yard to the Lubjek's garage, sat on the red car seat next to Ronnie, and watched as he hunched forward in the half-dark, elbows on thighs, and rolled a joint with his pale, freckled fingers. A white line of sunlight edged with yellow half-circled one of his knees. We smoked the joint, squinty-eyed and tight-lipped, holding the smoke in, then letting it out in clouds. When Ronnie exhaled the smoke in a rush, he banged his knees together, like he had to pee or something. There was just enough light to see him. His eyes were already pink-streaked and heavy-lidded when he turned to kiss me. I made out with him on the red car seat for a while, pretending we were in a house, our house, a house with cracks of light in the walls, our house in the world. *This is our house,* I imagined myself saying to someone as I stood in the dirt next to the door where thick vines of leafy green kudzu sucked onto the wood.

Ronnie stopped kissing me and fell to his knees on the ground, and I slid off the car seat next to him. We crawled on hands and knees to a scratchy blanket laid over the dirt, quickly undressed, and pressed our bodies together again. I held on to Ronnie's sweaty shoulders and stared at the dark beams of wood above us as he moved himself, *huh, huh, huh,* in and out of my body, thinking, *This is our house and this is what I'm supposed be doing. But why am I more interested in the cobwebs and the mud daubers' nests?* Late that afternoon I got Daddy to give me the car, and I drove over to see Cat.

I hadn't seen her in over two months. Every now and then I thought I heard the *bluhbluhbluhbluh* of her VW rumbling down Satsuma Street, but no. Nothing. Driving out of town, away from Chattahoochee, I felt myself growing calm, the way Mama must've felt when she got near water. I rolled onto Victory Bridge, thinking of the woman with the yellow shoes. How someone should've told her, *You don't have to jump off a bridge to go somewhere else; you could cross it instead.*

After a few miles, I turned down the road to Cat's house. It felt good to be out in the country, a rooster tail of red dust whirling in the air behind me. A row of dandelions grew in the grass along the edge of the ditch and when a sudden gust of wind blew, the air filled with hundreds of white, feathery seeds. I only had one wish. *To leave Chattahoochee.*

I drove up into Cat's yard, parked next to her bug, then got out and knocked on the door. No answer. I looked over at her mama's house. I could just hear the thin sound of a radio. Maybe she was over there. As I stepped off the porch, I heard Cat's voice. "Girl, I thought you were dead." She stood in the cool black shadows on the road, a bamboo fishing pole slung over her shoulder, a stringer full of catfish in her hand. When she got up into the yard, into the bright sunlight, she propped the fishing pole against a tree and laid the stringer of fish on the grass. Streaks of sweat ran down the sides of her face. "Thought your mama done went and drowned you for real," she said, wiping her hands down the sides of her jeans.

"No," I said, "but I think she would've liked to." I looked at the fish lying on the ground. Bits of grass stuck to their silver bodies. A fin moved weakly.

Cat rubbed the line of sweat on her cheek with a thumb. "She'd kill you now, if she knew where you were. You got a death wish?" She folded her arms across her chest. Waited for me to say something.

"No," I said. "I just got a wish." I thought of the cloud of dandelion seeds I drove through to get to this place. "I'm sorry you had to be there, to see how crazy she can be." I looked at Cat's smooth brown face, thought of the kisses I'd planted on her cheek.

"I don't want to cause you any trouble," she said. "I'd feel terrible if something bad happened. Not just to you, either. I don't want any crosses burning in my yard." She tugged my arm. "C'mon, let's sit on the porch."

I sat down. "She's not like that," I said. "Not burning crosses."

"According to people like her, I got two strikes against me, Lily. Three if you count being a woman. Hell, I'm out before the game even gets started."

"You don't feel that way about yourself, do you?"

"Hell no," she said. "I love me some Cat Reeves."

She laughed, then got serious, looked away from me, down the road. "You can't let some skinny old crazy woman tell you what to be."

I didn't say anything. *I was a fish once, blue as a boy.*

"Girl, you thinking too much." She sprung off the porch, picked up the stringer of fish, held them up high. "Come on in the house and help me clean these fish. I'll fry you up a couple."

She made everything seem so simple and true. I followed her into the house as if it were my own.

. . . . .

A couple of days later, Mama came home. James and I were eating lunch at the kitchen table when she walked in. She wore a new pair of sunglasses and a short sleeveless dress I hadn't seen before. Her arms and legs were tanned dark brown. Even her hair looked different, combed back over her forehead, pinned on one side with a silver barrette shaped like a palm tree. I thought maybe she was trying on a new personality, the way she had when she went through the wig phase, and I found myself wondering which person to talk to. I decided to talk to the person who'd left. "Call next time," I said. "We thought you were dead."

"Well," she said, standing next to her overnight bag where she'd dropped it on the floor, "I am dead. The me I was, I mean. I've made a decision. I'm leaving. I quit my job—already have another one."

"But you just got here," James said. "I'm pitching tomorrow night."

She put her hands on her hips and enunciated her words carefully. "I'm sorry, honey, but I'm leaving. Lea-ving. I just came home to get some of my things. I'll have to see you pitch another time." She turned away and went to her room. James and I stood in the door and watched her pack her clothes into the green suitcases she'd been given as a wedding present, the way we watched when she dyed her hair that time. I thought about what the counselor had said about getting out. And now she was beating me to it. Funny.

She plucked dresses off wire hangers, held them up and gave them a look, before throwing them into either the suitcase or into a pile on the bed. Some clothes weren't going because clearly, they didn't fit her personality anymore. She wasn't packing anything brown, that was for sure.

"Where are you going?" I asked.

"Winter Garden." She sighed. "Don't you just love that name? It's perfect." She held up one of her old cotton nightgowns, then wadded it into a ball and tossed it into the trash can. "I've traveled all over Florida the past few months, and Winter Garden is *the* place. You know, James, the Dodgers do their spring training at Vero Beach. That's not very far away from where I'll be. Plus," she said, "I've met the most wonderful man. His name is Henry, and yes, Lily," she said, twisting her head sideways to look at me, "he's the one who gave me all those carrots." She laughed.

I wondered if she knew how wacky she sounded. She was leaving, running off with a man named Henry, a man who courted her with homegrown vegetables, although she didn't call it that. Running off. "What about Mr. Kaufmann?" I said, thinking of how Daddy thought he was Mama's boyfriend. "Won't he be disappointed?"

"Oh God," she said, looking up at the ceiling. "You should give me more credit than that. Mr. Kaufmann is over eighty years old. We're just buddies—driving buddies. He introduced me to Henry on one of our trips. Henry's an entrepreneur." She rolled the word around in her mouth, then picked up a lime-green sweater, held it against her chest. "Honey," she said, looking at me, running her hands over the sweater, "you gotta admire a man who can grow his own vegetables, although you wouldn't care about that, would you?"

And then she left. I helped her carry her bags to the car. Mr. Kaufmann sat crouched behind the steering wheel of his blue Lincoln, his white hair slicked back, a can of beer between his skinny brown legs. Mama slid onto the seat next to him. She dug the pair of dark sunglasses out of her purse and put them on. "Good-bye, Lily. You'll tell your father, won't you?"

I watched as the Lincoln pulled away, Mr. Kaufmann hunched low in his seat, Mama riding high in hers. I wondered what it was that made her run after a new life after living the wrong one for so long. I was glad she was leaving, off to claim the life she'd dreamed of. She wouldn't be able to blame us anymore. I felt like kicking my heels into the air, breaking into song: *We're off to see the Wizard, the wonderful Wizard of Oz, because, because, because...* Mr. Kaufmann tapped the brakes at the end of the street, and the taillights flashed red. Then the car turned and they were gone.

. . . . .

When Daddy got home that afternoon, he wouldn't believe Mama really left. "Why?" he said. "Why did she leave?" He acted as if one of the butterflies in my cigar boxes had unpinned itself, folded its stiff wings, and taken flight. *Jesus, Daddy,* I wanted to say, she never meant to stay in this place. *She got stuck like everyone else. We were flypaper.*

For the next couple of days, he expected her to come home; in the afternoons, he pulled the sheer curtains back with thick fingers to look out the window. In the mornings, he cooked enough scrambled eggs to feed all of us before walking out of the house, jingling the keys deep in the pockets of his sagging khakis. "If I hold my mouth right, it'll start right up," he said just before stepping out the door. He sat in the old yellow Fairlane, hand on the ignition, praying for the engine to turn over so he could go to work. He looked like he was talking to himself. Always. When Mama was still around, we put jigsaw puzzles together, and Daddy would hold up a piece for all of us to see and say to nobody, "If I hold my mouth right, this piece will fit right there." It never did.

After Mama had been gone a couple of weeks, Daddy snapped out of his Rip Van Winkle state and realized shit had gone downhill. Everywhere. Next to the sliding glass door in the living room, dark green ivy had creeped in, running up the doorjamb, winding around the curtain rod like a rattlesnake. A corner of the parquet floor was crumbling into dust. The stove had gone black inside from spilt food. The cabinet beneath the kitchen sink was waterlogged and sagging. Every faucet in the house leaked. Daddy went out, bought a five-pound hammer and some nails, and fixed the screen door on the front of our house. It had been hanging off its hinges for months.

Yet nothing he did lasted. The screen door came unhinged two weeks after he fixed it. He put washers on all the faucets, along with new handles. Within days they weren't dripping but were running worse than ever. He cut the ivy off the curtain rod, pushed it outside, and closed the door all the way, but the ivy sprouted two new strands and worked its way back into the house. He fixed the cabinet beneath the sink, then waited for the wood to become waterlogged again.

It was too late. The house was like Mama. It had a mind of its own and couldn't be fixed. Crazy as she was, Mama had figured that out. A Jackie O wig or a box of Clairol Hot 'n Sassy just didn't cut it anymore. What she needed was a whole new life. When she hightailed it out of Chattahoochee, she scattered her old life to the wind like a box of cracked and peeling photographs she didn't want anymore.

Blown like leaves across the grass were the places where Maisey and I rode our blue tricycle, the trees we hid behind playing hide and seek. The azaleas we caught bumblebees on, the azaleas Mama crawled under later, humped over in the fragrant dirt like an animal. The ditch across the street and every drop of rainwater that washed through it, the wisteria that hung purple from tree-strangling vines, the creamy, white honeysuckle with its sugary drops of nectar, the black-and-white television we fought over. The bamboo jungle where James played soldier by himself, the black Naugahyde couch she sat on to roll her hair, every can of White Rain she ever used, the chair Daddy sat in to smoke, along with every match he struck. She threw away the hen and rooster she made from seeds, every chicken, duck, or turkey she made from Clorox bottles or pine cones, the photographs of us as chubby, hand-tinted babies, the kites we flew, the kites we let go of, the jars we caught lightning bugs in. And she threw away every fish we hooked and scaled and fried and ate, the lake we swam in, the lake I drowned in, the fights over my being the wrong kind of girl—a slut, a queer, a boy, the wrong person, the wrong daughter. She threw away almost everything.

37

One day when Maisey and I boxed up the bits and pieces Mama scattered behind her, we came across some old photographs. As I looked at them, they seemed to come to life like clips from a movie. I didn't want a mother anymore, but if I had, I'd have wanted the one I saw in the photograph Maisey found stowed away in an old green purse next to some of Mrs. Vanatter's poems. Inside the scalloped white edges of paper, Mama flirts with the camera, poses like a beauty queen standing in a small wooden boat on the shore of Lake Seminole, barefoot, hands on hips, head thrown back, a wide and bright smile. Open.

She's wearing short shorts, and the look on her face says: *This is how I want to be remembered; I am as marvelous as Miss America.* She gives herself to the camera. I imagine my father before he was my father, smiling at my mother before she was my mother. He has a head full of glossy black hair. Squinting his eyes, bringing her into focus, he snaps this photo of her, thinks of butterflies resting on leaves, camouflaged, right before they are netted, pinned into boxes.

Then there was a photograph taken after Mama had

children. May 1961. That's one year after Maisey was born: Now Mama has three children, and all of a sudden she's wearing shoes, as if she's afraid we're going to trample her feet. And we are. No more smiling barefoot Miss America. The photograph is blurry, hazy. She sits beneath a mimosa tree in one of those old-fashioned shell-shaped lawn chairs, scrunched to one side as if she's going to share her seat with someone much smaller than herself. Her hands are clasped on top of her head, her legs crossed. She smiles weakly. To her left is a clothesline, diapers fluttering in the breeze. In the corner of the photograph, there are bleary shapes, tiny feet, what seem to be hands. If you squint really hard, you can almost see one baby helping another baby stand.

. . . . .

Mama left, but her image stayed, burned into the velvety blackness behind my eyelids, like a flash from a camera. When I closed my eyes she appeared in full color, as if on a stage, a tiny version of herself. There was nothing else I could do but dream her into her new life. I had to do this; I had to get her settled before I could begin to dream my own life into being. What was on the other side of all those "if only's" I'd heard about over the years?

Some nights I closed my eyes and she swam up out of the darkness, climbed into Mr. Kaufman's Lincoln. I climbed in with her, watched as she rolled down Highway 27, past a blur of palmettos and scrubby pines, past giant billboards promising the Florida she always wanted: Weeki Wachee, Cypress Gardens, the St. Augustine Alligator Farm.

I could hear her voice above the wind rushing by, see

her turning her head, her hair blown crazy, to look at me perched in the backseat of the car like a crow: *See,* she said, pointing out the window, *Chattahoochee isn't really Florida. Not with all that red Georgia clay.* And she was right—Chattahoochee sat on the Georgia line—parts of it were actually in Georgia.

The farther south Mama rolled, the more of Florida she got; red clay gave way to white sand; oaks gave way to orange trees; I could see it all, and I wondered if she felt herself changing, too. I wondered what she thought as she stared at the palm trees whizzing by, if she thought her dream of being the queen of something was finally coming true. I fell asleep before I got my answer.

But I know this much. She moved into Henry's pink-and-silver trailer in the Seahorse Trailer Park on the edge of an orange grove. In her backyard, palm trees curved out of the ground, their bark scaly as snakeskin. She was surrounded by concrete seahorses; she breathed the sweet scent of orange blossoms.

She sent photographs to prove she was happy. She sat on the hood of a beat-up Cutlass holding an orange in her hand as if it were a small sun. She leaned against Henry in the blue shadow of an oak tree, smiling. I looked closely at Henry. He had a scraggly, black beard and he was whip-thin, reminded me of a greyhound. I could tell he was one of those dark-skinned men who drank Old Milwaukee and fished off piers in between jobs he could never keep.

In one of her letters, Mama told me Henry kept bees, and I pictured her standing in shade next to a row of gray boxes beneath an orange tree white with blossoms, bees swarming around her, the air heavy with their buzzing. I closed my eyes and heard a low drone. I dressed Mama in one of those beekeeper hats, hid her face behind a veil, placed a smoker in her hand. She always hated bees, afraid they'd sting her or us. I figured living with Henry must've really changed her. This was her new life. Still, it was hard to believe that she wasn't just visiting that place, that she actually lived there, surrounded by all those seahorses, all those orange trees, all that green.

She sent us a postcard of an alligator from Henry's store. The words she wrote on the back sounded like something a game-show host would say: *When Henry isn't tending his hives or working in the grove,* she wrote, *he runs Pete's Paradise. It's an open-air market like the ones we used to see on our way to Panama City. Remember those? Y'all used to beg your daddy to stop.*

I felt sorry for myself when I put that card down; I got sweaty just thinking about all that time me and James and Maisey spent being driven around in the backseat of the Fairlane, begging Mama and Daddy to *please please please just stop and let us out at Shell World, at Stuckey's, at Howard Johnson's.* I could still see the giant pink clamshell gaping open in front of Shell World; I could still see how it looked from the dusty rear window, getting smaller and smaller as Daddy drove away. I was ready to get into the driver's seat.

Mama said she could buy all the taffy she wanted at Pete's Paradise. She didn't have to tell me what was in that store. I knew. It was crammed top to bottom with jars of orange-blossom honey, ashtrays shaped like Florida, and coconuts carved to look like monkey heads. I could just hear Mama sighing when she opened the door. "Isn't it wonderful? My own little bit of heaven."

. . . . .

I never asked Mama how she met Henry, but from the pictures she sent it was clear he was as brown as she was, though, and I knew that wasn't a coincidence. She wasn't going to hide anything about this man now that she'd made her choice. I knew they cruised around Florida, lolling naked on sand dunes at secluded beaches, their skin coated with salt from the Gulf. I knew they ate shrimp dinners and slept in cheap motels with names like Stardust or Sand Piper. I figured all those souvenirs she'd brought us had come from Pete's and decided it didn't matter. I wasn't going to hold Henry against her. I was willing to let her have her life and didn't understand why she wasn't willing to let me have mine.

One day after school when I checked the mail, there was a postcard of a mermaid from Weeki Wachee. Maybe she'd sent it as a joke. *Ha! I beat ya!*

I flipped the card over to see what she'd written. *Thea the mermaid ate a banana and drank a Coke underwater—can you believe it?* I could tell you this much about my mother and the mermaid: When Thea swam into the spring, Mama leaned forward to watch as she drank her bottle of Coke, gulping the liquid down, her eyes open wide. When Thea peeled her banana and ate it, her jaws clenched, her mouth forced into a grin while she swallowed, Mama thought she was having fun.

Maybe that's what it was that day, the day I drowned. Maybe Mama forgot herself watching me sink into the green; maybe she waited for me to sprout a tail and swim off, a silver-tinted flash of something, something just visible in all that green. Maybe she thought of my birth. How she thought I was a fish baby. Maybe she thought, *If drowning could be like this.* I would never know what she thought that day or all the other days. I closed my eyes and pictured myself saying to her all the things I could never say while she was there: *I was a fish. You let me drown. I wasn't a fish. I was a boy. I wasn't a boy. I kissed a girl. I was a virgin. I kissed a boy. I kissed another girl. I am your goddamn queer.* Even though I said these things a thousand times, I could never make her say, "I know."

. . . . .

One night, months after she left, I fell asleep and dreamed of Mama. She sat on the muddy bank of the Apalachicola River, her cane pole arcing out over the river. Her eyes had a soft look to them, and she seemed to be whispering something. For the life of me, I couldn't figure out what it was. The wind caught her voice like a kite and shot it high up in the air out of my reach. It seemed as though she was saying something serious, something that might change my destiny, something other than the story of my blue-and-silvery fishbirth. Or my drowning. Then Mrs. Lubjek arrived, took one look at Mama, read her lips, and turned to me laughing, speaking the words so I could hear them. "She wands you to geb her another cand of worms."

That dream was the last time I saw Mama while she was still alive, and I could believe it was really her, that she actually showed up in my head. She was killed in an accident driving home drunk from the beach. It was just that simple. She left us and she died. When I heard the news, it wasn't really news. Like Daddy said after she shaved her head that time, she was one surprise after the other. In the end, nothing she did was surprising. Not even getting killed when she was finally starting her real life, the one she'd imagined for so long. I wondered if she thought of her new life that way—as her real life, as if the one she'd lived with us had just been a bad dream. I wondered about the difference between a real life and an imaginary one. Which one is real? The life we imagine for ourselves or the one we actually live? I thought of Rae and Ronnie then, how the straw houses, the shack, and Ronnie's garage were imaginary. I'd imagined a self to live in them. Then I thought of Cat's porch. I remembered how alive I felt lying on that porch beneath the stars, everything imaginary stripped away. I knew then that I didn't want to wait like Mama had, to live my real life. I wanted it now.

· · · · ·

We had a simple funeral at Mt. Pleasant. I thought about getting Mama one of those concrete markers with a number on it, but I didn't think anyone else would appreciate the joke. She would have, I think.

After it was all over, after all the flowers from Nichol's Flower Shop, all the lilies and the roses and the carnations, wilted and turned brown on her grave, I tried to picture Mama, tried to remember what she was like before, when she still dreamed of being a beauty queen and driving that convertible Cadillac. When she had babies one after another instead. When she held me in her lap and softly murmured the story of my birth into my ear, her breath warm against my skin.

But I found that I couldn't even remember the sound of her voice, the way she called me home at dusk, turning my name into a song, Lil-ly, Lil-ly. She was already fading, color draining out of her like a photograph left too long in the sun. I couldn't remember how she looked in her white cotton nightgown, either, leaning over me and Maisey at night, nibbling words into our ears, *Mmmmmmm, I love you.* Her breasts brushed against the sheets as she bowed her body over our bed. I couldn't remember her smell, whether it was the delicate scent of Johnson's baby powder or the sweet almond smell of Jergens lotion.

I couldn't remember how she looked asleep or how she looked when she woke or how she looked in her white uniform when she tiptoed into our room to kiss Maisey and me good-bye before she went to work at the hospital. I couldn't remember the shoes she wore or how her feet looked or what dresses she owned, her shorts or her shirts or her sunglasses, her favorite color or whether she even had one. I couldn't remember her walk or her run. *She wanted to run away from you,* James said. I couldn't remember how she sat in a chair or stood to talk on the phone. I don't know who she would've talked to. *She told the women she worked with that you were pregnant,* said Maisey.

I couldn't remember the exact brown of her eyes or how long her eyelashes were or how her lips were shaped. I couldn't remember her fingernails or the palms of her hands, how it felt when she slapped me. I couldn't remember how she sounded calling me a goddamn queer long before I knew it myself. I couldn't remember how she looked underwater, her red hair floating above her head in all that green.

I couldn't remember how she looked when she caught a

fish, peeled a potato, or drove our car. I couldn't remember how she looked hanging our clothes out on the line, bending over the basket to grab a shirt. *You were supposed to help her because you were a girl,* said James.

I couldn't remember how Mama looked walking through a Jackson County farmer's field picking White Acre peas under the hot summer sun or how she looked later at home sitting on the porch, shelling them into a big, green bowl.

I squatted at the end of a row and peed in the soft brown dirt while Mama stood over me and I stared above at the bleached-out sky. That was the moment I knew the Earth was round; I could see it curving away from me, the way Mama curved away from me as soon as I was born.

ABOUT THE AUTHOR

Lu Vickers received her Ph.D. in English from Florida State University, where she was a Kingsbury Fellow. She has twice been awarded Florida's Individual Artist Grant for fiction, as well as an Emerging Writer's grant from the Astraea Foundation.

Vickers' short stories and poetry have appeared in *Apalachee Review, The Gay Community News, Journal of Florida Literature, Sundog, Kalliope, Calypso, Common Lives,* and more, as well as the anthologies Love Shook My Heart II, Women on Women 3, and others. Her essays have appeared in several magazines and Web sites, including Salon.com, HipMama, and the St. Petersburg Times.

She lives in Tallahassee, Florida.

ACKNOWLEDGMENTS

THIS NOVEL TOOK a long and leisurely drive along the scenic route before arriving home at Alyson Books. It began its life as *Snap*, a collection of interrelated short shorts inspired by the late Jerome Stern who originated the contest for the World's Best Short Short Story contest at Florida State University. And like the snapshot from which it took its name, the collection slowly developed into something else. A lot of people helped me along the way. Thanks to my mentors, Sheila Ortiz-Taylor, and Jerry Stern, whose voice I can still hear. To the friends who read and critiqued early drafts of the novel: Bucky McMahon, Mary Jane Ryals, Deborah Kay Ferrell, Meri Culp. To my book club, especially Heather Montanye, who insisted I share my work. Special thanks to friends Mary Jo and Michael Peltier and to my family, my brothers Bill and Crisp, my sister Melissa. To my parents, who made me into a writer; you are long gone but not forgotten. *Mahalo nui loa* to my friend Pam Ball who read the novel a hundred times, always with a fresh eye. A surreptitious thanks to the Aphrodisiac Queen who rolled over me like a tide, giving and taking away. To my agent Alison Picard, who believed in my work and gave me a chance. Special thanks to my editor, Shannon Berning: thoughtful, professional, enthusiastic. Every writer should be so lucky. The following organizations provided support: the FSU Kingsbury Fellow committee, the Florida Arts Council, TCC and the Astraea Foundation. Finally, thanks to Jennifer, who makes everything possible, and to my three boys, each and all better than any word I'll ever write.